Faultline

ALSO BY C.M. BANSCHBACH

The Dragon Keep Chronicles
Oath of the Outcast
Blood of the Seer

The Drifter Duology
Then Comes A Drifter
A Name Long Buried

Spirits' Valley Duology
Greywolf's Heart
Saber's Pride

Drax Guard: Crew Six
Flashpoint
Faultline
Conduit
Stoneheart
Shrike

Fates Defiant

FAULT LINE

DRAX GUARD: CREW SIX #2

C.M. BANSCHBACH

Faultline

Copyright © 2024 by C.M. Banschbach

All rights reserved.

No portion of this book may be reproduced in any form without written permission from the publisher or author, except as permitted by U.S. copyright law.

NO AI TRAINING. Without in any way limiting the author's [and publisher's] exclusive rights under copyright, any use of this publication to "train" generative artificial intelligence (AI) technologies to generate text is expressly prohibited.

ISBN: 979-8-9890651-2-7

Published by Campitor Press

clairembanschbach.com

Cover Design: Emilie Haney @eahcreative

Drax Guard Logo: Morlin Lorenz @thatmoonysky

For my fellow middle children.
We're criminally underrated.

1

Besim

Whoever says family is easy, never met mine. I stand outside my sister's coffee shop in Dunhare, Oregon, hands tucked into jacket pockets against the crisp late winter wind that's doing its level best to keep us indoors.

It might also just be an excuse to keep my hands hidden for a few minutes longer. I'd never thought myself especially vain, but the warped burn scarring across my left hand, arm, and part of my cheek tends to draw eyes and weird glances. Like my height didn't already do that.

Perks of being a half-troll.

All trolls look human, except for the aforementioned height—I've never met a full or half-troll under six feet—and the skin. Dull silver and holding a toughness like granite. Stoneskin shattered more than one weapon back in the days when trolls were more bloodthirsty and feared and did more earth-rending.

But I'm half, so I've got normal human skin, a warm brown from my mom's side, and it comes with a trick. Come danger, the stoneskin appears, giving me an added protection that sometimes beats the chain mail or armored tac vest I wear on missions with the spec ops Drax Guard.

Another wind gust whips around the corner and tries to invade. I shrug my shoulders, pulling the coat tighter. My collar is flipped up, and like my hands, I've got an excuse for that so long as I stay outside. However, I have to go in, and I'm not sure I'm ready to deal with the way eyes have been looking not at me, but at the scarring etching its way up my neck and smattered across the lower part of my jaw.

Get it together.

Guess I am vain. Something to admit to the next time one of my seven siblings teases me for being the perfect kid. I shrug my shoulders again and step inside *The Fox and Ground*.

Warmth and the cheery scent of cinnamon and coffee hits. Two elves with pointed ears and bright green-and-silver eyes sit across from each other, laptops open. A human hunches over a textbook, protein bar wrappers stacked beside her coffee cup. A full fae with vibrant grey eyes has earphones over his pointed ears, nodding along to music as he types. There's someone new behind the register, and the exits are still clear. My hand curls in the safe confines of my jacket pocket.

It always takes time after coming back from a mission to stop being on edge when I step inside a building, or even just outside the garage apartment I took over years ago at my parents' place. But coming back from the last mission on a stretcher and spending two weeks in a hospital bed delayed that processing time.

Or maybe lengthened it too much. The rest of my crew hasn't said anything. But maybe they haven't noticed in the last month since I got discharged. I don't know if I'm relieved that they haven't noticed I'm off-balance, or wishing they would say something.

"Hi, welcome in!" The cheery voice of the new employee alerts me to the fact that I've been standing there a few seconds too long and I can't really cover by pretending to study the menu. I'm still at the door and a good thirty feet away from her.

I stride over, hands still in pockets.

"What can I get started for you today?" She meets my eyes, wavers once towards the scarring, and I'm tempted to scratch at my chin to cover it. Her dark eyes have a striking grey band around the iris, brighter against her black skin. Most likely pointed ears under the curls. Her eyes aren't fully grey, so half-fae. Grey is the most common eye color when it comes to fae. Purple is the other and denotes Britannic ancestry.

I shove hands down further, threatening the seams of the dark jacket. "I'm actually looking for Nadire."

The barista gives me a new once-over, caution there. It makes me pause. It's like she's trying to make sure I'm not a threat.

I take the non-scarred hand out and jerk a thumb at my chest. "Brother."

Her features clear and she offers a smile. "I'll go get her."

I check the view behind me in the shimmering surface of the espresso maker. Still clear, and the bell hasn't dinged for anyone else. Patrons are still in their spots, computers open and headphones in, even though the speakers are playing some sort of muted instrumental music. It sounds like Nadire raided Mom's music closet for the Albanian sound Great-Grandmother brought over to the Allied States.

The clock on the wall in the midst of painted vines and knotwork foxes and bears nodding to our dad's old Norse bloodlines tells me I've got plenty of time before the rest of the crew shows up. Enough time to try to talk Nadire out of whatever insane thing she's got planned next. Or turn her computer off then back on again to fix whatever tech issues she's panicked over.

Her text wasn't very forthcoming on information. Just a *-get over here.-*

Which is not really what you want to tell your big brother who's been serving in the Allied States Armed Forces since he was nineteen and has been in the special forces Drax Guard for the last four years. Texts like that make my mind go right to breaking some jerk's arm.

However, having lived alongside Nadire for all of her twenty-five years, I know she's got a tendency for the dramatic and it's likely nothing. I should just be glad she's kept in contact with me.

She's always been the hot-headed one in the family, the one most likely to cartwheel her way into questionable decisions. This coffee shop is her most recent endeavor and is a point of contention between her and our parents. The rest of us have our opinions, but some of us are keeping them to a minimum around her to make sure she still comes around for family dinners once a month.

Blessed are the peacemakers.

"Hey!" Nadire comes out of the back, sweatshirt sleeves rolled up to expose the twining tattoos covering her forearms. She doesn't have the stoneskin from Dad like I do, so her tanned skin will take the tattoo and not fight back against the process.

Guess it takes wild magic to burn through the protective skin provided by our troll DNA to eat into the more easily damaged human skin. My hand tightens, pulling again at the new scar tissue.

"You want a drink?" she asks, jerking me back to the café and away from leaning dangerously back to the Wastelands mission.

"Depends. What do you need?" I return.

"What, I can't invite my sibling to my coffee shop just to chat?"

I arch an eyebrow and she relents, acknowledging that I know I'm here for something and it's not a one-on-one conversation. At least not yet.

"Okay, the computers are acting finicky again. I thought I'd call you first instead of the tech guy who installed them and probably ripped me off."

"In that case, I'll take a coffee."

A gleam enters her brown eyes. "Can I make you one?"

My lips purse. "What kind?"

"A new kind I've been wanting to try." She snaps fingers at me. "Maya came up with it. We're going to make it and you're going to drink it."

She darts off, pulling the half-fae employee from behind the register to help.

"No peppermint, you know that's disgusting," I call, but they're already bent over the counter. I leave before I can see what she's concocting and head to the back office.

It's a mess. Sorry, *artfully arranged*. I straighten the sea otter calendar on the wall, flipping it to the correct month as I do. Piles of paper, and what look like a few applications with the shop logo at the top—a knotwork fox leaping over a steaming coffee mug. I shuffle those into a pile and spend a few more minutes just sort of pushing things back into place before sitting down at the computer.

The seat's comfortable and re-covered with a hideous mustard-yellow cloth. Probably to hide whatever was on it when she hauled it out of storage—the only place she'd find a chair cheaper than zero dollars and that would fit the children of a nearly seven-foot troll and a six-foot-one human woman.

I tap the keyboard and the screen flickers to life. A family picture appears. I can't help but smile faintly back. It's from two Christmas Eve's ago and we're all in hideous sweaters, piled around Mom and Dad. We'd taken it hours before I'd gotten the call from my old sarge just as we were coming out of Midnight Mass. "Gear up, it's time to go."

The Drax Guard comes before family, and my crew is a different kind of family. The ones who know the sides of me I'll never let show around my seven siblings and parents and few friends outside the crew. Every time I'm home on leave and working on the newest construction site alongside Dad and my oldest brother Enver, I get the not-so-subtle questions of when I'm going to leave the Army behind and settle down.

To which I give the answer of when it's time. I'm only twenty-eight and not about to start a life in the family construction business when I still have brothers in the field.

"Okay." Nadire barges in. "Maya is finishing up. What's the diagnosis?"

I spin the chair to face her. "That this office is a mess."

She frowns and points to the computer.

"What am I looking for?" I ask.

Nadire huffs and plops down on a rolling stool. "Sorry, forget you're not actually a mind reader. It's been running super slow and glitching on me."

"Did you install the program I told you to?"

She hesitates a telling beat and I turn back to the computer, calling up the history and seeing what I can find among the code, and starting a download for the program to scan for viruses in the background.

A knock announces the drink. Maya tries to find a place to set the cup but the desk is covered. I reach for it instead, and she hands it over.

"Maya, this is my heroic brother, Besim. He's Drax Guard and a huge freaking nerd."

I huff a laugh. "Nice to meet you, Maya."

She flashes a grin. "You too. Enjoy." And she's gone.

"New employee?" I ask casually and I can *hear* the eye roll behind me.

"Yes, and I even called her references and ran a background check." The sarcasm doesn't get me to turn around.

"Doesn't hurt to be careful, Nadi," I say, and she scoots the stool over to better scowl at me.

"I know what I'm doing."

"I never said you didn't, but—"

"Oh, what. Is she going to steal the invaluable secrets of coffee making? She's new in town and needs something part-time while going back to school. Satisfied?"

"You know it's my job to be suspicious."

"You could try turning off the soldier brain every now and then," she mutters.

"Being protective of a sibling is not the same as stifling dreams," I return gently.

A sigh cuts from her and her shoulders slump. "I *know*." The words and expression are mulishly accepting.

I try the coffee and get a warm, nutty flavor. "This is good."

Nadire allows a smile. "Told you it would be."

"Technically you didn't tell me anything. You adding it to the menu?"

"Maybe. I'll test it on a few more people before trusting your opinion. You'll drink anything."

This time I scoff, turning back to the computer to start coding in extra layers of security and making it easier to track sales from the register and having them appear automatically in an accounting program.

"You should have just asked me to set all this up in the first place."

"Didn't want to ask for anything else." The dismissive voice has me looking at her. She's propped elbows behind her to lean on the desk, and stares at the sea otters clasping paws.

"Hey." I tap her arm gently with my elbow and it gets a faint smile.

"You were gone for over two months on some top-secret mission. Wasn't sure when you were getting back..." Her eyes stray to the warped skin on the side of my neck before jerking away.

It was easier in the hospital when I was doped up on pain meds and antibiotics, healing magic buzzing under my skin and through my veins as my entire family crammed into the room to see me. But the injuries had been covered by bandages and it was easier to take the looks. Now, it seems like they're all tiptoeing around me and the reddish scars.

"I'm fine," I say sharply, and immediately have to acknowledge the irony. Cieran lost it on us on the mission after we'd been asking him if he was okay again and again. I'm starting to understand the frustration and the way it can just slip into anger in a split second.

"I know." She's almost as good at the "therapy voice" as I am. That's what Dejan calls it, and he always scowls more when I pull it out.

"Hey." She scoots closer, keeping an elbow on the desk. She looks a lot like Mom, a softer roundness to the broader troll facial structure, the same smile in the corners that prompts a room full of laughter. Her hair has a bit of wave and is always in some sort of disarray or haphazard bun.

I take a cautious sip, not really looking at her the way she wants me to.

"You can come by whenever you want. I won't ask questions or anything. I can figure out dumb stuff to talk about if you want, or I don't have to bother you at all. None of us really know what you do, and I don't really want to, but you've always got us."

A faint smile tugs my mouth, and I meet her open glance. "Thanks."

"You're welcome." She lightly punches my arm. "Now what's wrong with my computer?"

2

Besim

Twenty minutes later, the computer runs at full speed with a few extra security features and an easy-to-read FAQ so she doesn't have to call me if she doesn't want to next time. Because there is going to be a next time.

I've still got half a cup of coffee left, so I take it and meander back out. It's warm enough in the shop, but I'm keeping the excuse of patrons in and out and giving the winter chill an ingress point for keeping the jacket on.

Guess I really am that vain.

The rest of Crew Six should be showing up at any minute. I take a seat at a raised table over by the wall. Its four chairs are easy to get in and out of, no way to be boxed in. You know, should anything remotely dangerous happen at this coffee shop tucked in among businesses and some other shops outside of downtown Dunhare.

Corporal Dejan Kostic is first in. The blond elf slides in through the entrance, avoiding ringing the bell. His thick jacket hides a knife strapped to his forearm. He's not wearing one openly on his thigh but it's probably in with the jeans loosely tucked into his half-laced military boots instead. Ballcap backwards over short hair, highlighting the pointed tips to his ears.

He tilts me a nod across the room, and goes to order a coffee. Maya helps him, and then in comes Nadire.

"Hey, Dejan." My entire family knows the crew, and we've been here a few times since its opening six months ago. "Hey, you're from Detroit, right?"

I sip my coffee, watching the subtle change come over Dejan whenever Detroit is mentioned. A slight stiffening in his shoulders and a forced smile.

"Yeah."

"So is Maya! She just moved in."

But Maya's got the same look, a lot more clearly warily sizing Dejan up. Interesting. He doesn't really talk about his past in Detroit. Most of what I know about him is the last four years serving in the same Drax Guard crew as our medic and archer, the few years of service in the regular enlisted forces before that, and his paramedic service before that. He's technically the oldest of us despite looking like one of the younger. Elves.

Another thing I know about him is he always uses cash, doesn't make friends outside of us, and doesn't like very public places. But then, I just described over half of the Guard.

He joins me a minute later, relaxing once he's across from me. "She's new?" He inclines his head back to the counter.

"And theoretically got a background check and references called and everything."

He smiles slightly, picking up on the wryness. Another thing I know about him is he's just as protective of my family as I am. Even though I'm pretty sure he almost stabbed someone the first time I brought him over to family dinner with all ten of the loud, hug-loving Antilles clan.

"Should I be surprised your head's still intact?" His light green eyes shot through with silver brighten with amusement.

I arch an eyebrow and incline my head slightly, which gets a light chuckle. My eyes flick toward the door as it dings again, bringing with it Specialist Remy Kalama, our third brother. Like us, he prefers to wear the heavy boots even outside of missions, but he's just in a lighter hoodie despite the cold. He's a warlock—human with innate elemental based magic—carrying the intense fire magic of his Hawaiian heritage, and cheats with it to keep warm on cold days.

Nadire greets him, practically shoving Maya out of the way. Dejan snorts softly as he leans on the table and watches. She's got a crush on Remy, and he's pretending to be blissfully ignorant of it, because he stonewalls every woman who tries to flirt or express interest. Dejan and I don't know his ex. She'd been around right when we all made it into the Guard together. And then she disappeared without a word, showing up later to dump their newborn kid on him and vanish a second time. He was definitely different after that.

I need to just tell Nadire—again—to back off, because I know Rem's not interested. But I'm also waiting for him to just tell her. Though with the way he's being polite and chatting with her, no more than basic updates, he's not doing it anytime soon.

He waits another minute at the counter to take the cup of hot water and added tea bag, and grabs Dejan's coffee before joining us. He takes the lid off and gives the bag a little bob before leaving it to steep. He's always joked that being three-quarters Hawaiian and a quarter Britannica from his mom, tea is the only option for him. He'll drink coffee on missions, but he looks penitential doing it.

"He coming?" Remy asks.

"Last I knew," I reply.

"He been okay?" Dejan turns his cup between his hands.

"Last I knew." I lift my shoulder.

Remy tugs the bag string again. We're waiting for number four. Cieran O'Donnell, sergeant, and potentially the newest member of our team. He was discharged from the hospital before me, but he's also still dealing with the emotional fallout of losing his old team sixteen months ago. Then his sister to cancer four days before we went out on the Wastelands mission that got him brought back on a stretcher too.

He's been around a few times in the last month and a half, but still hasn't taken the commission the Drax Guard CO has stayed one paper short of ordering. Not that we blame him.

That's part of what this meetup is. Seeing if he'll show, and if he's made a decision. The three of us agree. We don't really want a different sergeant to take over the crew, not after the Wastelands. And we need an officer to keep going on missions. Because Dejan doesn't want to keep filling in on team-ups with other crews like we did a few times after our old sergeant Pothos Allaire moved to the reserves months ago. And we're not getting split up.

Remy taps a finger against the rim of his cup, and the steam whisking off the top calms immediately. "How you doing, Bes?"

Dejan turns the same look at me, the unyielding one asking for a real answer instead of a shrug and "fine" that seems to do it for everyone else. I'm honestly not used to it being turned on me, since I've always been the one to truly be fine, the one looking out for everyone else.

And I don't like that the tables are turned, that I feel like I'm not competent enough to take care of them, to be the rock to be leaned on.

So, "I'm fine."

Remy arches an eyebrow. He's confessed his fear that he's not a good father to his three-year-old mischief maker, but he's got the dad look down. Dejan just hums into his coffee, and the sound grates against my nerves, fraying them slightly.

Again, the rough irony of this happening after I pestered Cieran about the same things on the mission is not lost on me.

Thankfully the chill rushes back in, bringing the sergeant with it.

He makes us, and there's a slight hesitation before the nod. Nadire slides off from where she'd been casually sitting on the back counter.

"Hey! You haven't been here in a while. Good to see you again!"

Cieran keeps his hands tucked in the jacket that's open over his hoodie, and returns the greeting. "Yeah, found my way back over here."

"Plain coffee?" she asks and at his nod, she continues, "Sure I can't make you something different?"

He chuckles. "Sorry. One of these days, maybe."

She turns to Maya and tells her, "Plain black coffee with a bit of caramel."

"Name?" Maya asks.

"Cieran." He pulls out his wallet, but Nadire's eyes go wide.

"Wait, *that* Cieran?" she asks, and points to us.

He follows the look and then swings back to her. "I'm scared of what that means." He half-laughs.

"I figured you were military, but didn't think you were—" She knows enough not to yell *Drax Guard* in the open café. "Um...on the house. Honestly."

"No, I can't," Cieran tries, but she's shaking her head.

"Least I can do after you took care of my brother."

I offer her a slight smile as she looks my way again.

"It was more them looking after me," Cieran says, and tucks a bill into the tip jar instead. "Thanks, but last time though." He frowns and she nods, giving a smile back.

He takes his coffee and heads over, sliding onto the empty seat next to me, frayed holes in the right knee of his jeans exposing his prosthetic lower limb.

"Sarge." Remy nods. Dejan tips his chin up.

"Thought I was going to be early," Cieran says. His ballcap is on backwards too, compressing dark hair. Circles linger under his eyes, and he leaves his phone face-down on the table, exposing the heartbond dampener around his left wrist.

The other half of his heartbond is dragonwalker soldier Athina Spera, one of the four-soldier fleet we met and allied with on the mission. They'd tracked a sorcerer from the Kirnae Archipelago in the Atlantica Ocean over to the American Wastelands. The same terrorist who'd killed Cieran's old crew a year and a half ago.

The others catch the dull copper glint at the edge of his hoodie sleeve.

"They still haven't decided?" Dejan asks.

Cieran's fingers go to the bracelet, spinning it around. Athina left with her team three weeks ago after they were all cleared from the hospital, but there's ongoing discussions between our two countries and military on how to handle a heartbond—and mental connection allowing for mind-speak—between two members of the respective special forces teams.

"No, other than we can keep in contact via phone and these have to stay on for now." He shakes his head slightly. He's ticked off, and I have no doubt she is as well.

"I'm sure that's going over well," Remy says.

Cieran huffs. She's been the one to help him start pulling himself out of the mental pit he's been stuck in for months after losing his entire family, blood and otherwise, and for that reason alone, we like her.

"Yeah."

"Doing okay?" I ask. He looks like he hasn't been sleeping again.

Remy and Dejan give me a "seriously?" look I ignore.

Cieran just spins the bracelet one more time and closes his hands around the coffee cup. "Outstanding." We need a towel to wipe the dripping sarcasm from the word.

"Anything we can do?" Remy beats me to the question.

Cieran leans on the table, arms braced and hands rotating his cup around. "Maybe just get the question out there." He glances around. He knows why he's here, and it's not for some social call.

"You going to take the posting?" Dejan speaks. He's blunt, unafraid to ask the question. But after years of missions and slowly nurturing a friendship with him—he's cautious around new people, and usually that comes out as antagonistic. Whatever he did or was before, he must have gotten burned pretty bad since his first reaction is to get anyone to show true colors.

And the way he stares Cieran down, he's doing it right now. He agreed with us when we talked it over—we don't want a different sergeant, but he's still not certain about Cieran.

"You sure you even want me to?" Cieran slumps against the table. "I really didn't do that great of a job on the mission. Got caught, stabbed, had to rely on you guys to save our asses."

"That's what a team's for, Sarge." Remy flashes a faint smile. Cieran just frowns at him.

My hands curl around my cup of lukewarm coffee. I could ask Remy to get it back to hot in a second—nothing's ever stopped me from handing him a cup the way he just hands me electronics to fix. Magic and electronics don't usually jive together, and the more powerful the magic is, the more things tend to fritz. Though recently it's been three-year-old fingers causing more issues than magic.

Maybe Cieran needs to hear this from them instead of from me, the guy who was bugging him the entire mission. But it's still rankling in the most idiotic of ways that they're beating me to it. Me who usually has to nudge each of them to talk to anyone outside of the team. Remy buffers Dejan's sharpness, and I mediate between them and everyone else since Remy doesn't go out of his way to befriend many people either.

Dejan's attention flicks to me when I shift on my chair, a question in the tilt of his eyebrow. I shake my head, taking a sip of the coffee. I should just push it over to Remy, but instead I'm stubbornly clutching it. Wow, great. Trying so hard to be fine I'm just going to be stupid about things.

"It's just..." Cieran darts a look around, then spins the heartbond dampener. "I don't know if I can or should. I felt almost back to normal for the week and a half she was around, and then they left and I've got this." He tilts his wrist. "And I feel like I went backwards, pushed back past any progress I made, and..."

He manages to look at us again before focusing on the spot of table between his arms. "I don't think I'm good for this anymore. I'm thinking about finally taking a discharge." The last words come hushed, directed at the table.

It punches us all in the face.

"What?" Remy stares at him. It takes any of us in the Guard time to trust, but Remy was instantly fine with Cieran taking lead. Dejan just shakes his head, like he knew all along this was going to happen. A faint tightening at his jaw and around his eyes marks how disappointed he is.

And me? I'm...angry. Saints, I'm really angry. My hand tremors around my cup and I stare at it in horror.

"Didn't think you were a quitter." It slides out before I can stop it and then I've got all three of them looking at me like I got snatched by a sorcerer and swapped for a mimic. Cieran's eyes narrow and he's still got the sergeant look, assessing, weighing.

I can't look back, focusing instead on my cup. Can't apologize either, the way the anger still swirls. *What is wrong with me?*

What I'd meant to say was more along the lines of "it's okay to still be grieving." It's barely two months still his sister passed away, and sixteen since he lost his crew to the terrorist we took down.

Or Athina did. I was too busy getting burned alive by wild magic. And the thought conjures another restless shift at the memory of fire scorching through my stoneskin, eating away at me, leaving these strange fractures inside me.

A jingle of the bell sends all of us glancing that way. We dismiss the man—elf from his ears and height just shorter than the average human, eyes bright green and silver—but Cieran stiffens, fingers of his right hand curling and reaching for his left sleeve and the knife hidden there.

Remy clears his throat, jerking Cieran's attention to him. I've only got a profile view of the sergeant, but there's a sort of wide-eyed feral-ness to him right now.

"Who's that?" Remy asks in a low voice. Dejan leans closer, tracking the guy as he makes it to the counter and orders in a low baritone. He's wearing a knee-length jacket over a bulky sweater, styled dark brown hair, and some sort of designer boots meant to look like work boots.

Cieran's fist turns white-knuckled. I forget my stupidity and reach over to nudge his arm with a fist. He jerks a quick breath and relaxes like he wasn't about to attack some guy in a coffee shop.

"That's one of Andrej's guys."

The quiet words hit us all differently. Andrej. The sorcerer terrorist who killed Cieran's old crew, and is now officially dead from being bitten in half by a dragon.

Remy brushes his fingers over the table-top, tracing a rune. He taps his fingers on it, then returns to cupping his tea like nothing happened. But now, we've got a low-level silencing ward around the table that turns our conversations into indistinct murmurs for anyone trying to listen in. Especially elves who have hearing twice that of a human.

"I thought everyone was taken care of?" Dejan watches the guy, taking a sip from his coffee to mask some of it.

"I guess not." Cieran's laugh is sharp and bitter. "He was one of the lieutenants in the organization. He was at the hideout in the Wastelands."

"You sure?" I hate to be the one asking it. But grief can do funny things. Suddenly I'm back to being more logical.

Remy gives the same apologetic look, mirrored much more subtly in Dejan's face.

Cieran huffs again. "I don't need this stupid memory to have all their pictures still burned in my head from months of tracking and fighting."

Photographic memory. And one that rarely steers him wrong from what I know of him from years of service and some crew team-ups on past missions. He grabs his phone and taps for a second before tilting it my way. He's dodging the sergeant posting and thinking about discharge, but right now is still okay with giving a silent order.

I pull out my phone, log into the secure Guard system, and run a search on the name he gave me. It takes thirty seconds before hits start coming in. And keep coming. But top are the arrest pictures and crime list from when this guy got caught three years ago. Still got perfect hair in the mug shot.

I place my phone in the center of the table. Remy and Dejan glance at the photo and nod. It's him. Damien Janvier. Elf with Nordic ancestry. Sorcerer marked, which means he's supplementing his natural magic through illegal means—be that stealing magic items, siphoning from another magic user or natural magic well, use of blood magic or any magic classified as "dark," or just dealing any of the above in black market deals.

Another few skims through more information and it's confirmed—known associate of Andrej, lieutenant in the terror organization which might not be as dead as we thought.

"We taking him right here?" Dejan asks. He's pretty stabby for a medic.

"Yeah." Remy snorts. "In a coffee shop full of civilians when he hasn't done anything yet. I'll come to your trial," he offers.

Dejan's mouth flattens, but he's not offended. Cieran, however, is still stiff, watching Janvier.

"I'm not finding much on current activity." I keep my voice low, feeling settled back to myself to do my job. "I'll need to get to the tower and on a computer."

That claims Cieran's attention and it lands on me and then the others. Dejan stops his observation long enough to give him a nod.

The sergeant might be thinking about discharging, but if this guy is still linked to anything remotely suspicious and Andrej's old organization—we're going to bring him down.

3

Besim

"Can you get a tracker on him?" Cieran asks Remy.

The warlock takes a sip of tea, glancing sideways toward the sorcerer. Then he shakes his head.

"Not without him noticing." He looks apologetic. "He's ranked second class, and he's looking at us right now."

Second class. He's powerful. And if that's in his file then someone either found out the hard way, or it's a guess. Either way, if Remy says he can't, then best leave it be. Warlocks are the lowest ranking for magic users, being human only, and usually only going through trade-school training to harness and use their magic. A lot for jobs like construction, welding, firefighting, and the like. Anything an elemental based magic might be useful for.

Or, like Remy, for combat. He might not have a degree in magic to bump him up to the wizard rank, but he's one of the most powerful wielders I've seen.

"Okay, head out in pairs," Cieran says. From the glance he gives to Janvier, he doesn't think it's a coincidence he walked into this coffee shop on a day when we're all here.

If it is a coincidence, then some saint snatched the threads from a Fate and is weaving like mad.

"Rem, with me."

Remy nods and caps his tea, scooping up the discarded tea bag and tossing it into the nearest wastebasket. He scuffs his hand through the invisible rune and the noise of the coffee shop increases slightly. Cieran and Remy head off, talking more loudly about "the game." Which leaves Dejan and me.

And our elf is back to watching me. I shove back from the table before he can say anything, feeling the sharpness of his gaze as I start to head out.

"Besim!" Nadire's voice makes me wince. She doesn't know there's a terrorist in her shop, doesn't know we were trying to leave to get more intel. And doesn't know that if Janvier is looking for something, she just gave it to him.

But I can't ignore her now. I pivot and she looks to me with brown eyes soulful and almost wary.

"I'm serious," she says. "Come around whenever you need."

Have I always been this annoying with the same offers and support? Hearing this feels like knives squealing against my stoneskin. And it's heightened by the sudden hug she gives me.

Maybe she feels how I instantly stiffen, because it doesn't last long. And when she looks at me again, her concern is not masked very well at all.

"I'm fine," I say. "See you around."

I head for the door before she can say anything else. Outside in the blustery cold, I shove hands back into my pockets. Dejan jogs a few steps to catch up, and I slow a half beat to accommodate his shorter stature. Even if he's at the tall end for an elf, I still tower over him by half a foot.

He doesn't say anything, just has hands in his jacket, but I can feel the questions and comments. He's also pretty judgmental.

"What?" I finally growl.

Dejan just lifts his shoulders and keeps walking. Until I stop. He moves a step ahead before reflexively pivoting. He tips his head and arches an eyebrow.

"What's bugging you?" he asks.

"You need to work on your therapy voice," I say after several frustrated seconds, but he sidesteps to block my intended step forward. I glare and he stares back unperturbed.

"Talk to me, Bes."

"Talk to you?" I snort. "You never talk."

"And you're never this pissy." He still blocks my way.

"I'm. Fine." I've definitely felt like punching him before, mostly when he's being extra stubborn, but this time it feels like I might do it. And that's scaring me somewhere deep down under all the swirling irritation and anger.

He just grunts and steps aside. Oh, he's not accepting it, but thankfully he's not pushing right now. We finish the walk to the command tower in silence. He doesn't complain or fall behind when I unconsciously lengthen my stride. He's not even breathing hard when we get there, even if he was practically jogging the whole way.

I do feel a little bad. But apparently not enough to say anything.

The Allied States Army base takes up a quadrant of Dunhare. The city's grown around it over the last two hundred years. Dunhare started as an army outpost when a civil war turned allied against a sudden invasion of fire drakes. And it was from here that four soldiers from both sides of the previous factions had banded together and made the strike at the volcanic nest, blowing it.

No one predicted the volcano would go supervolcano when it mixed with the natural magic reservoirs and all the magic thrown around in the war. The fire drakes were wiped out, but so were a quarter of the States, leaving a swath known now as the Wastelands draped north to south across the country.

Those four men started a legacy of special forces, now the Drax Guard today. We step inside the Guard's command tower that sits on the edge of base. The entry floor is mosaiced with our symbol—a bloody fire drake coiled around a sword. *Fear No Fire*, the Drax motto curved underneath the image leaves an ashy taste in my mouth. Two months ago, I didn't. Two months ago, I wasn't afraid of much.

We pass the wall of honor with countless names etched in stone. Cieran's old team is on there. Pictures are framed all around it. Memories of the men who've died in the line of duty. No wonder he hasn't really been around much in the last sixteen months—imagine walking by your dead crew's names every day.

Dejan sticks with me as I head to a second-floor tech room to grab a laptop, and then back out and up to floor three for a briefing room. Most everyone else is on-duty soldiers in dark grey fatigues, a few in street clothes like us.

Usually people will at least say hi, or offer a nod, but something's got them walking right on by, some with a raised eyebrow. And it takes a few minutes and three missed conversations that usually happen before I realize...it's me. Dejan's been the one to reply with a word or gesture. Though, maybe that's throwing them off too.

That pokes again.

"Dej!" A stocky elf stops him in the hallway. Ylan glances my way. He's part of our deep cover division, and he and his team have been undercover for five months in the city. Even I don't know their mission.

Ylan tilts his chin up. "Hey, big guy." His slight Texas accent still sneaks through no matter what mission he's on.

I manage a "Hey, Ylan," and make a point to look down from the half a foot I've got on both elves. Dejan smirks faintly, and indicates I should move on. Ironically, I'm going to be the one waiting in the room and Dejan's going to be the one talking in the hall.

I just grip the laptop and slide past them, heading into a briefing room at random. The others will come find me.

It's definitely warmer in here, so I shuck the jacket, not stubborn enough yet to die of heatstroke in the tower. But also slightly more comfortable knowing the others won't be staring at the scarring with eager questions in their eyes.

I stare fixedly at the screen and refuse to glance at my hands as I start working up a more comprehensive briefing on what we have on Janvier. Last known locations or sightings, associates, and a long, long rap sheet.

I'm so focused, I miss Remy's entrance. It's only when I reach for the cup of coffee that's not there that I look up and see him. Rem slouches in a swiveling chair, tilting it side to side with his foot sprawled out in front of him. Arms crossed over his chest and eyes closed as he rests his head back.

I want to ask. Ask how he did it. Over a year ago when he got caught crossways between a spell and his counter-spell and got hurled fifty feet, body smoking and half-conscious during the fight raging all around. After that he'd been fine. Business as normal. Joked about it.

Rem's an honest sort of guy, easier to read than an open book, and something like that apparently didn't bother him. So what's wrong with me?

"Anything on the way over?" I ask, mouth feeling dry.

"No sign of a tail," Remy replies, not opening his eyes. "We walked the whole way. Apparently, Sarge hates buses."

Complaining like he doesn't love being outside, especially on sunny days when he basically soaks up sunlight like a battery to keep fueling his magic.

I...can't really confirm we didn't have a tail because I hadn't been paying attention. A wince almost makes it out to my face. I keep working instead, pulling together a facial search from security and traffic cameras citywide, comparing it against Janvier's mug shot. Hopefully he'll have been caught somewhere and we'll figure out how long he's been in the city.

Our database also links to a few others like the Federal Bureau of Investigations, and the Bureau of Magical Affairs. I set up another search to run in the background. It'll at least let me know if they've got any open cases tracking him. We'll have to make a call to get any details, since cases are usually locked from outside access. And if there are some, we'll either be handing this over to the investigating party or having to work with the Bureaus. And that's going to be annoying for everyone.

When I look up again, Dejan's in the room, sitting across the table from Remy. My crossed forearms brace against the table, shoulders hunching as I keep staring at the computer. Waiting for them to say something.

But maybe that's just always been me. Bothering everyone so much that I'm ignoring myself. Or maybe waiting for someone to check on me instead.

Except the times they have, it's made me defensive.

But I'm *fine.*

Remy glances my way, and I beat him to whatever he's going to ask me by turning it to Dejan instead.

"What did Ylan want?"

Dejan has a scrap of paper from somewhere that he balls up. He flicks it at Remy who catches it, sets it on the table, and flicks it back. Sometimes I think I'm dealing with my teenage siblings.

"He and his crew are trying to infiltrate some gang. He wants more guys. I told him I don't do boring work." He aims the paper ball at Remy's hands now propped like goal posts on the table.

It skews left and misses. Dejan jerks his hands up in protest. Remy smirks and grabs the ball. It's teenage siblings with magic. Usually I'd be halfway watching, halfway dodging whenever they inevitably turn to tossing magic around for bigger trick shots, but something about life as normal has me sinking deeper into my slouch, arms pressing harder against the table, staring unseeing at the screen.

Until something taps my forehead and the paper ball falls to the keyboard. I glance up, irritation simmering again. They're both watching me, still relaxed in their chairs.

"What?"

"Did you not get your twelve hours of sleep last night?" Dejan asks. I frown and toss the ball back. A bit of light green magic snares around it with a lift of his finger and it veers midflight, speeding toward Remy who catches it in cupped hands like he caught a fifty-yard spiral.

He's given me sarcasm and I can use that. "Only eleven."

The door creaks open and Cieran steps through. "Sorry I'm late. Ran into a fossil in the hallway."

Our old sergeant Pothos Allaire follows him in, and Dejan releases a rare smile. Pothos is in dark grey fatigues with the ASA patch on the right shoulder and Drax Guard patch on the left. Dark hair peppered with grey cut close, and mismatched eyes from a mission long before he got the three of us, when his magic got tangled up with a fae's and left him with some unique additions to his warlock powers. The left eye is vibrant grey from the fae magic, and the right is his natural green.

"Hey, Sarge." Remy extends a hand and gets a quick clasp and fist bump. Pothos circles around and drops a hand on Dejan's shoulder, lightly shaking him. The elf smirks and offers a fist.

"Besim." Pothos gets to me. "These two haven't killed each other yet. Well done."

"Thanks, Sarge." It gets a smile from me. Dejan and Remy have been close since our first mission when Remy punched him and Dejan immediately stopped goading.

Cieran takes the chair at the head of the table, back to spinning the bond dampener around his wrist. Pothos drags a chair out by Cieran and sits.

"CO's on his way. You got anything yet, Bes?" Pothos asks. Like he didn't shift from active duty to desk job a few months ago. Like he's still our sergeant. Maybe some part of me is still upset he did even though he had perfectly good reasons to. Like patching things up with his wife and making sure he was around as his kids keep growing up.

"Still running some stuff down." I tuck my left hand underneath my right elbow, continuing to hide it the way I can't quite hide the scarring on my neck.

Pothos came to see me in the hospital. He knows. But sometimes it feels like the forty-two-year-old sergeant who got stuck with the younger twenty-somethings for the last few years of his active-duty career is more like a dad or surrogate uncle and I don't want to disappoint him either.

Which is stupid. He's seen me laid low once or twice and has never blamed me for anything tech related going wrong.

Dejan and Remy fall to chatting with Pothos, catching him up on everything. Remy's inviting him over sometime for dinner, see his kid who's affectionately nicknamed "Bear." Cieran watches it all, a wistfully sick expression on his face.

We've tried—actually it's been more Remy and Dejan who've tried—to get Cieran out and about again since being discharged from the hospital weeks ago. But each time, he's gently stonewalled. It's easy to see he's still not okay, but this time I'm not closing the gap like I did a few months ago.

A soft alert chimes from the computer and I'm glad to focus back on that instead of the mess inside. No open cases on Janvier, which is concerning until I see it noted that he's presumed dead. Someone must have been crossing fingers since he hasn't been sighted for over a year. But Cieran confirmed his presence two months ago at Andrej's Wastelands hideout.

Another alert dings. This time louder, and conversation rumbles to a stop. I feel their focus turn to me, but I'm still scanning data and compiling some of it in another document for easier access.

Footage for the last four months has been scanned. There's a few brief shots of the side of a head about a month ago that *might* be him. Then more hits start coming in and it's all in the last three weeks.

He's all over Dunhare, sometimes with another man or two close by, sometimes by himself. The last hit comes in, five hours ago, full facial view as he waits at a cross street.

I freeze the frame, and turn the computer around. "This morning, Parkington and Eighth."

Cieran stills, glaring at the computer like he can leap right through and stab the guy. "That's two blocks from Shay's house."

"What's over there?" Pothos asks.

"Nothing, just residential houses."

"You think he's following you?" Dejan asks. He and Remy are both alert, leaning on the table, ready to go.

"I haven't seen him face-to-face until this morning," Cieran replies. "What else came up, Bes?"

A very childish "I thought you were taking a discharge" almost escapes and I hunch my shoulders more, flickers of shame creeping in that I'm wanting to act this way.

"Cameras have been picking him up all over the city in the last three weeks. Before that, it's debatable if it's even him. No open cases on him right now. And full links to Andrej's organization, though it's been about a year since he's been actively spotted. I might have to adjust some search parameters," I admit.

"Where's he been in the last week?" Pothos asks.

I tag the camera footage and start listing off cross streets and days and times. A low curse interrupts after the fourth data point.

"I've been within two blocks of all of those sightings," Cieran says. Now he's really peeved.

"Revenge?" Remy asks.

Cieran huffs. "I don't know. I don't remember any specific run-in with him, but my last two missions involved the terrorist organization he's in. I don't know, maybe he's sad Andrej is finally dusted."

I flash the same grim smile as the others.

"From all reports, the organization was pretty gutted after you boys cleaned up the Wastelands," Pothos says. "Maybe he's looking to rebuild. Take out the guy with the highest success rate against them, or get the glory of killing the guy who took down Andrej. Score some points with new followers."

"Technically it was Athina. I was busy getting stomped on by a chimera shifter." Cieran gives a poor smile. I dig my middle two fingers into the base of my thumb, keeping me from diving back into those chaotic moments of pain and fire.

A sharp rap at the door announces Captain Bron Wolfe, Drax Guard CO. He's already waving us back down as we're halfway from our seats to salute. He's in the same grey fatigues, hair cropped shorter than we all keep ours, a bit of grey frosting through his. He's been around for a long time, and has got one of the best service records in the last fifty years. Usually friendly, can be slightly terrifying if ticked off, but someone you know will have your back no matter what happens.

"Sergeant." Wolfe levels it at Cieran with a gruff daring. Maybe Cieran's already tried to talk to him about discharging. It's something Wolfe would understand but would try to get him to stick around for longer. Cieran's one of the best we've got too, and losing him to wounds like that would suck.

Cieran's greeting is lower, and he quickly turns his attention back to the heartbond dampener. Wolfe's hand clamps on his shoulder for a second before he passes by and acknowledges the others.

"Sounds like we've already got something." Wolfe gives a slight shake of the head as Pothos leans forward, and focuses on Cieran instead. The younger sergeant takes a second to realize the CO's attention is on him, and he startles slightly when he does. Almost deer in the headlights.

"What do we have, Sergeant?" Our CO is relentless.

Cieran swallows hard and lifts a hand to indicate me and the computer. "We saw Damien Janvier in a coffee shop this morning. Confirmed associate of Andrej and one of the top lieutenants in the organization. Besim has been running searches. All sightings within the last week have been within two blocks of where I've been."

"You sure it's him?" Wolfe asks.

Cieran gives a mirthless smile. "I remember every single one of those *sunkatas*, sir."

Wolfe softens slightly. "What else have you pulled up, Besim?"

I give him the same updates as I did the others—no active cases, but a few more attributed crimes have populated from the search still running.

"Okay, sounds like he might be targeting, otherwise it's a very coincidental crossing of paths for the last few weeks. And you know what I say about coincidence."

Smirks flare all around. We do know what he says and it's not very complimentary.

"Cieran, I want you running this with Crew Six."

Cieran lifts his head again, lips thinning in a line, but he doesn't argue. We were all there to see Janvier and he doesn't technically have a crew.

"I want you staying on base or at the tower," CO keeps going, but Cieran's shaking his head.

"If I'm bait, we get him faster." A wince creases around his eyes as he says it, and he tugs the dampener again. Guess that made it through to Athina and she's probably not thrilled about it.

Wolfe picks up on it. "We going to also have an issue with a dragonwalker?"

Cieran moves his hands apart, pressing palms to the table for a moment like he's trying to suppress everything. "No, sir."

"Might be easier if he takes it off, sir."

We're all surprised at Dejan's comment, the way he says it unperturbed.

Wolfe frowns. "Know much about heartbonds, Corporal?"

Dejan shrugs, and whatever it was that had him chiming in vanishes. "Just what they taught us in paramedic school."

Wolfe studies Cieran and then Dejan again, sharp eyes not missing much. "Cieran, you're not going out without at least one of them with you, preferably a magic user. Pothos, you're backup only if needed."

The gentle reminder has our old sergeant smiling ruefully, and all four of us disappointed by the way we all shift slightly in chairs.

"We need a lot more intel before we start anything. Besim, see what else you can dig up and try to establish any pattern for the last week, if not more. Cieran, you're staying here for now." He softens slightly. "Call your girlfriend, tell her you'll be on mission."

It feels like a weight is left out in the open. Tell her he'll be on mission and hopefully nothing's going to go sideways. But Wolfe's not going to jinx anything.

"Sir." Cieran's hands twitch like he wants to pull his phone out immediately.

"You three, alternating shifts every five to six hours to start. Remy, you're first up with Cieran."

Another round of acknowledgments.

"Route updates through Pothos, but any plan or actionable intel comes to me for approval. We're in the middle of the city here, and I'm not interested in unleashing another terrorist attack."

"Yes, sir."

He stands and we all do the same. "Good luck."

Pothos lingers behind after Wolfe leaves. "Let me know if you boys need anything. Listen to your sergeant." He claps Cieran on the shoulder, but the younger sergeant isn't chuckling like the others. Pothos keeps his hand in place, and nudges Cieran toward the door. Shifting into dad mode as they leave.

Hopefully he'll be able to talk some sense into Cieran because I apparently won't be able to. The thought spears irritation through me.

Since when is it *my job* to do that?

I slap the laptop closed and gather it up, facing off with Dejan and Remy as they move away from the table.

"You need me to do anything, Bes?" Dejan asks, and it's almost cautious. That kills the irritation, and chagrin fills its place.

"No, I'm just going to be staring at a computer screen."

He grimaces. "Think Cieran's going to have any different orders?"

I shrug.

Remy sticks hands in his hoodie pocket. "Think he's really going to do it?" he asks.

Dejan carries the same disappointment a little better. "Something tells me this mission is going to be the deciding factor."

I push my thumb around the corner of the laptop, over and over again. Realizing this might be our last mission together doesn't help anything I'm feeling. Or trying not to feel.

Either Cieran takes the posting, or we get reassigned into different crews. Unless one of us takes a promotion none of us want. Even then we'd still be dealing with someone new coming onto the team to round out the fourth position. And we'd still prefer it to be Cieran.

"I guess we go find out." My index finger indicates the door.

Cieran leans against the wall outside, phone to his ear, boot scuffing the ground. Pothos has already moved on. Maybe there wasn't some sergeant-to-sergeant talk.

"I know," Cieran says softly. He shakes his head. "No, they're not going to let you do anything if you do come." A faint smile creases. "I know you can." He chuckles. "Chill, hot stuff."

Remy drops to a crouch, balancing on the balls of his feet as he leans against the wall. Dejan slouches, hands in his pockets. I tuck my arms over the computer, widening my stance into something more comfortable as we wait.

Cieran glances up, losing any levity. "Yeah, I have to go." He clears his throat and straightens with an effort. "Got three idiots staring at me right now. Yes, I will tell them you say hi and that you'll incinerate them if anything happens to me. You're so sweet."

But a grin creases his face again, and Remy and Dejan are smirking. Remy mimes a gag, and Cieran kicks at him.

"I know. Love you too."

This time both Remy and Dejan retch and Cieran flips a gesture as he hangs up. He tucks the phone away and his hand settles at his hoodie collar like he's gripping an armored tac vest instead.

"You need anything, Bes?"

It's about the mission but it still drives the nagging feeling back. I shake my head like I can dismiss it with the action.

"I'm just going to find somewhere more comfortable to start digging." I tap the laptop.

"Sweet. I'm going to find something to punch. Remy, you want to come protect me from the scary training room?"

"I'd be so honored, Sergeant." Remy pushes to standing.

Cieran rolls his eyes, coming back to himself. "Dejan, what are you doing?"

The elf doesn't shift his hands from his pockets as he pushes from the wall. "Well, my options are bothering Besim while he tries to work, or bothering you two. Unless you need me to do something interesting."

"Yeah, head back to the coffee shop and see if you can pick up any trace or tail." Cieran's attention flips to me. "Bes, get him a list of the confirmed camera hits in the last few days. If there's nothing at the shop, head to each location and see if there's anything you can piece together or any other cameras or protective charms he might have triggered. I'll make out a list of what I was doing those days too, and we'll go from there. I want you on comms."

Dej flicks a small salute and we all shift to action.

4

NADIRE

I watch my brother leave, frown twisting my face. He's not *fine*. But that is what's throwing me off. I've never seen Besim *not* okay. Even after being in the Army for as long as he has, even coming back from some longer tours overseas or missions he won't say anything about, he's always been okay.

Guilt creeps in immediately. Maybe he hasn't been okay and has just been pretending this whole time and no one has ever stopped to make sure because it's *Besim* and we've never worried about him.

I slouch back against the stainless-steel counter, arms tucking over my stomach, feeling breathless.

"You okay, Nadi?" Maya's voice pulls me back, and I circle around the counter to join her behind the appliances and stacks of mismatched ceramic mugs, and the neater towers of paper cups with my cheery fox and coffee cup logo that I designed.

"Just suddenly very worried about my brother," I admit. It's probably not appropriate for an employer to be spilling to an employee, but Maya is about my age. Actually my age since the human side cuts the fae four-hundred-year life span to something more normal. Something that kind of makes me more comfortable around half-fae since thinking about living for four hundred years is...a lot. And Maya's definitely more reliable and centered than some of the late-teen/early-college kids who work the later shifts. I'm not talking to them about much other than shifts and school schedules and making sure they're staying on top of classes.

Oh crap. I just sounded like Bes.

"Isn't he the reliable one?" Maya asks.

A brief laugh escapes before my arms smother it in my chest. "Yeah. Usually. Which is why I'm suddenly concerned."

"He seems nice," Maya offers when I don't say anything more. I dart a look over. She has hands stuck in her barista apron, slight tilt to her head.

"Besim?"

She smirks slightly. "No, his friend you seem to really like."

I glare as my cheeks heat. Remy Kalama has never really given me the time of day. Not for lack of me trying, or Besim trying to get me to drop it. I don't even care if he's got a kid. He's just a really solid guy, and yes, I've had a crush since he first walked through our door with Besim four years ago.

Maya chuckles and straightens the laminated sheet listing our winter specials.

"We don't have to talk about it," I say.

"No, let me live vicariously through you," she complains good-naturedly. "I don't know anyone here and school is kicking my butt, so it's takeout and studying and serving coffee that's not overpriced." Her expression shifts to glare at me for my lack of charging the same as other shops around Dunhare.

I just want to keep prices as cheap as I can before having to increase them. It's always annoyed me to pay so much for coffee, but now as a businesswoman, I get it. And price increases are going to be happening a lot sooner than I want, or else I'm eating through my savings faster. And I really want this to last.

"Have you been talking to my family behind my back?" I shoot back, but the same little irritation flares through me. They all think the café wasn't a great idea. Heck, Besim might even think that, even if he's been outwardly supportive.

I owe him a lot more than experimental coffee flavors for fixing the computers. Maya arches an eyebrow and I smile apologetically.

"Reassure me that you have annoying family members who might be well meaning but really sound a little demeaning?"

Maya's shoulders drop slightly and she looks down, shifting her ankle-high boots against the tiled floor. "No, just one who's always getting into more trouble than he can handle."

"You want to join me in the 'worried about siblings' club?" I ask.

A smile returns to her face, wry this time. "I think I founded it."

I dig my phone out of my back pocket. "Then I'll be the snacks officer."

She laughs and I start a group text with all the siblings sans Besim.

-Hey, anyone talked to Bes recently?-

Astrid is first to respond. Almost instantly, as always. She's fourteen months younger than me and is an accountant at a really nice firm. And someone I'm *not* asking for help with books or finances just to get told how I'm doing it all wrong.

-Just in passing after Mass on Sunday. What's going on?-

Enver is next. I check the time. Lunch, so break time on whatever site he and Dad are working today. *-No.-*

That's so helpful. As usual.

-He picked me up from school yesterday and didn't say anything.- Taron, the youngest at fifteen, and somehow has a phone after we all had to wait until we were sixteen at the very least.

But that's exactly my point.

-He came by today with the crew, and just was...off.- I bite at my lip as someone else starts typing.

-I haven't seen him since the hospital, and it's harder to get a read over texts.- Kirsten, oldest and married with two adorable kids. It's not as easy for her to be around, but she and her family still come to most monthly dinner nights.

Which...I check the calendar. That's on Sunday. Four days to decide if I'm going or not.

"Hey, sorry to interrupt."

I glance up from the phone to see one of the customers standing there. He's got an expensive looking dark blue jacket over a cable knit sweater.

"Couldn't help but overhear." He gestures to his pointed ears. Elves have twice the hearing and vision as humans. Or half-human/half-troll.

I flash a tight smile. So glad that conversations are free-for-alls.

"But I had a brother in the military too." He gives a small shrug and a really charming smile. "And those guys kinda look like my brother did. I just wanted to say it's normal to worry about a sibling. He seems like a good guy, though."

My smile comes more naturally. "Yeah, he is." Something the elf said catches up. "Did?"

He softens into something sad and smaller. "Yeah. Didn't make it home a few months ago."

I swallow hard. It's the fear we all keep stuffed down every time Besim leaves, and we shove into a deeper corner of the closet when he comes back. "I'm really sorry."

"Thanks." He offers another smile and it's less vibrant. "Damien Janvier." He extends a hand.

"Nadire Antilles." I return the handshake.

"Nice to meet you, Nadire." He releases my hand and gives a slight bow that somehow works with him. "This is a great shop. I'll probably be back around if you need someone else in the 'worried about siblings' club."

I laugh. He left a really nice tip when he got his coffee, so for that alone I'd be glad to have him back.

"Nice to meet you too, Damien."

His eyes twinkle as he winks, spins on his heel, and leaves the shop.

"Doesn't hurt that he's easy on the eyes." Maya's elbow digs into my side. I shush her and lightly shove her away. She laughs, and goes around the counter, picking up a cleaning bottle and cloth to start making a sweep of some recently vacated tables.

I turn back to the phone in my hand, struggling to remember for a second what I was even doing before. Kirsten's text is still the last one. Right. Besim.

-Maybe we can have a sibling dinner sometime soon?- I wince. That sounds sort of needy. *-For Besim, just to check on him. He hasn't seemed himself since the hospital.-*

I brace for some comment from someone like, "Now you want to do dinner?" or something. I don't know. It's not like I'm on bad terms with anyone. Just...terms. I'm somewhere between dreamer and intense doer, and sometimes that drives my family up the wall. Add in really independent and it sometimes leads to some friction. Always did growing up, and still does now that we're all grown.

But maybe once I get really on my feet with the café, it'll make things easier. Have something to show and be able to stand with my other overachieving siblings who've done things pretty effortlessly.

-That sounds great, Nadi! Everyone sound off with a day that works for you.- Kirsten already taking charge. Maybe it'll be easier to just hand this one off to her.

A low-level headache has suddenly sprung up, humming at my temples. Great, just what I need now. I huff and turn back to the café. I'm going to end up needing a lot more customers to justify even turning the lights on today, much less tomorrow or the day after that.

5

BESIM

MY LAPTOP IS DOING all the work, and I'm on a low couch just waiting for it to give me the next burst of information. I lean forward on my knees, pulling out the small wooden rosary that lives in my jacket pocket. It's quiet in the small corner I've set up in, perfect for getting in a few prayers without interruption. But I can't start.

I just stare at the beads as I run them through my fingers over and over, the smoothness not coaxing me into any sort of prayer state. It's usually what calms me, centers me. But here I am, unable to ask anyone for help. And it's not like I'm blaming God or the saints, or even the Fates like some people like to focus on, for what happened.

I'm just here and trying to figure out which part of me broke and why.

"Hey." Cieran drops to the seat beside me. I didn't hear or see him coming, further proof that something's really wrong with me. "Sorry, am I interrupting?"

I shake my head. "Hadn't started."

He slouches back and tilts his chin at my hands. "Shay was a lot more religious than me. One of the families who fostered us growing up got her going to church. She was baptized and everything. St. John's."

I nod. That's the parish my family attends. I'm hard-pressed to remember his sister being there, but it's a big church.

"You ever think about going?" I ask, fingers rubbing across the beads again.

He shrugs, hands lacing loosely together. "I went a few times with her, toward the end." His throat bobs. "But hard to want to when life's been just a string of shitty things happening. Javi used to say that's how it is, but..." He shrugs again. "It gave her some peace about a lot of things, especially at the end. Can't fault it for that."

This is progress, him freely offering to talk about his sister and a crewmember, and doing it in a quiet way.

"No sage proverb for me?" Cieran half-chuckles, almost like he wants one.

I slide the rosary away and clasp my hands together. "You want useful or vaguely inspirational?" I ask.

He huffs another laugh. "If I wanted inspirational, I'd just go to someone on the street. You know I'm the *firren* inspiration, right?"

I tilt a look.

"Yeah." He raps his right knee and the hollow sound of the lower limb prosthetic rings back. It's a perfect replica of his lower limb, fused to the skin and nerves by the warlock prosthetists and elven surgeons. "Got my team and half my leg blown to hell but here I am walking and talking and pretending to be whole, so put me on a poster, right?"

"What's your catchphrase going to be?"

He rolls his eyes, but there's more life than earlier this morning. "Life sucks."

"That's really inspirational. Great for kids to hear." I nod and he shoves at my shoulder. I barely rock to the side under the force, but it gets a faint, maybe even real, smile from both of us.

"So what am I saying instead?" There's a hint of challenge, and I look away from it, and down to the healing scar tissue mottling my left hand. I don't really have anything to say. Usually I've got something. At least some sort of reassurance.

"I don't know. Maybe life does just suck." It slips out. Guess a bit of trauma broke my filter down to nothing and I'm just saying the first things to pop into my head.

But Cieran just makes some sound approximate to a laugh. "Yeah."

I curl my hand into a fist and shift so my right hand stacks atop it, hiding the scarring from view.

"Sorry about what I said earlier in the café. You're not a quitter." I manage to look at him.

He turns a thoughtful glance back from where he still slouches against the wall. "Seems easier though."

"Easier is almost never better," I rejoin.

He nods slowly, focusing on something across the room before blinking and glancing back at me. "Anyone ever tell you it's really annoying when you're right?"

A grin tilts my mouth. "All the time."

"Well it only took seven years and joining the Army last time I lost someone to get my head on straight, so guess I'm just getting started this time."

My throat tightens. He's lost everyone. Parents and a brother as a kid, a crew who was like family, and then his sister. He's got every reason to be a mess. I just had a few injuries and feel like I got absolutely pummeled, without any right to feel that way.

"You talked to Athina at all?" I manage to ask. Keep it on him. Do the one thing I might still be good at.

"Yeah. We talk, figuring out time zones and restrictions and heart-bonds and heartbond dampeners." Cieran slouches forward on his knees. "This isn't the way heartbonds are supposed to work, right?"

"So why didn't you ask her to come?"

He lifts a shoulder. "She's…" He sighs and taps his hands together. "I don't know. I just don't feel like it's right to dump her with all…this." He jabs a thumb at himself.

"Cieran." Okay, I've still got the "mom" voice. "She didn't run in the Wastelands and she's not going to run now."

His shoulders brace like he's going to deny it, but a chime from the laptop saves him from saying something stupid. I grab it and start sifting through the new data.

Cieran straightens enough to look at the screen too. "Sorry. Didn't mean to dump all over you. I came to see if you have updates."

"Update is you need to actually talk to your girlfriend."

"Hilarious."

"I try." I don't shift my focus. I'd widened search parameters, and now am getting more information and links to case files from several years ago. All confirmed involvement from Janvier and confirmed terrorist activity.

I skim through one case that a quick password entry gives me permission to view.

"So weird how people didn't buy 'equality in magic' after they tried to bomb the San Francisco bridge," Cieran scoffs.

"You on the case then?" The dates are two years ago.

"Yeah. That's about when we started active tracking and pursuit." He points to a grainy crime scene picture. "That's Masood." A wistful smile takes over.

It's a profile view of the Arab-American elf, thick beard obscuring half his face, sunglasses on, and tac vest on over jeans and a long-sleeve shirt. He's standing on some rubble, looking down at someone crouched below, bow and arrow at the ready. He was always a lot more friendly than our team elf, more gregarious and first in, last out on a prank.

I keep reading, more pictures coming up. The rest of Cir's team and some local police pushing handcuffed suspects toward cruisers. One of Cieran, hat on backward, tac vest on and broadsword at his belt, sunglasses on, pointing toward something on a crumbling wall with a Bureau agent standing nearby.

"They left signs everywhere," Cieran says. "Statement or whatever manifesto they were peddling. Usually had some sort of tracker information, so if someone knew how to get through the spell, it'd give them the location of the next meeting. One raid and then every sigil had a dozen different meeting places keyed in."

"How'd you finally catch up?" I close out the file—all trace magic was linked back to Janvier—and open another. It's similar, and this time, it's over in Celtica. Some standing stones by a ley line that got halfway decimated in what authorities think was some magic-gathering spell. Whatever it was, it left a lot of historians furious the landmarks were broken, and ticked off the fae who draw wild magic right from nature and magic reservoirs like ley lines. It'll take years to renew itself, and will reduce casting ability and potency of any fae in the area until it's back to full strength.

"He'd holed up in the mountains, right by the Columbia River. Ylan actually was able to infiltrate." Cieran nods pensively. "Was able to get a tracker on one of his guys, and barely got out before his identity got burned. We followed out into the Wastelands, and then…" His hands lift and I know the rest of the story.

"I don't ever really remember tangling with Janvier though." He indicates the new picture—some surveillance about two years ago. Looks like somewhere in Aegypt.

"Well, everything is showing him to be just as powerful and intentional as Andrej." I reluctantly give the report.

But he's not tied to anything Andrej was doing over on the African mainland or dragonwalker archipelago, so no reason to call the Kirnae fleet back over. No reason for Athina to come other than to help Cieran's sanity.

"Dej didn't pick anything up at the café or at those cross streets you gave him," Cieran says. "He's still out doing one more sweep just in case."

"Where's Rem?"

"Something came up with his kid. I told him to go and that I'd stay here." He pulls out his phone and checks it. "Made it back five minutes ago."

"So I'm on babysitting duty?" I ask.

"Why do you think I came to find you?"

"I thought it was for updates?"

"Look, I'm just a poor, traumatized sergeant who might be about to go outside and join Dejan in scouring the city for this *shilsa*."

"Am I supposed to stop you or join you?"

He flashes a smile. "My underutilized common sense says to probably stop me unless I want Wolfe to actually discharge me."

My brief laugh seems forced to my ears, but Cieran doesn't flinch.

"You got anything else? Anything that can help us pinpoint where he's coming from?"

"I'll set up an algorithm to organize the traffic camera sightings. I'm getting permissions for a grocery store camera, and some of the office building security cameras along those streets, but might have to actually *go* there to get some recordings."

He hums thoughtfully. "You should be able to get into our old case. Andrej had a few hideouts or bases round Dunhare and at least one known over in Portland. We hit each of them, but no joy each time. No idea if Janvier would head back. Some other gang has probably tried to take them over." He rubs his forehead creased in thought. "One was under the Forty-Second Street and Allstreet Avenue bridge."

I key it in and...no active traffic cameras in the area. Convenient.

"Might have to go get a visual on it," I report.

"Ylan might know." He skims through the contacts on his phone and hits call. "Hey, yeah it's me, your drug dealer."

I shake my head.

"I'm coming for your kneecaps." Cieran chuckles at whatever Ylan shoots back. "I've got an old acquaintance in town. You or your guys hear anything on a Damien Janvier?"

He listens and then looks to me. A quick search for alternate names comes up empty and I shake my head.

"This guy is so confident he's apparently never used any aliases."

Cieran scowls and passes it on.

"He might be looking for a reunion." He pauses. "Yeah. Someone we used to know had a lovely house under the Forty-Second Street bridge. Heard anything?"

He rubs his chin, nodding with whatever Ylan is saying. "Yeah, food truck on Fiftieth, seven hundred hours. Got it. Thanks."

Cieran slides the phone away. "Okay, he's sending one of his team over to monitor until tomorrow and then you and I will go get the report and some killer breakfast tacos." He checks his watch.

"There's been no other hits in the last few hours," I say. "He might have gone to ground."

And hopefully we didn't lose our chance to get him.

"He's planning something," Cieran says like he read my mind. "He's going to pop back up soon. Hopefully it's something we can stop in time."

6

Besim

It's two minutes to seven as Cieran and I make for the food truck. My laptop is in my backpack, and we've both got knives hidden under jackets and in boots. My longsword and his broadsword are a little too noticeable for the public, but Cieran has a two-inch-wide leather band on his left wrist that hosts a compressed shield. One tap to the raised circle in the center and it'll turn to a rounded, rune-reinforced buckler.

Sun's breaking through some cloud cover, and early sunbeams give faint spots of warmth. There are a few other figures clustered around the truck, breath pluming as they rub hands and chat amongst themselves, waiting for whatever amazing-smelling food is coming from the truck. It's puffing smoke and has only three tacos to offer from the chalk sign out front.

"Who we looking for?" I ask.

"He'll come to us," Cieran returns. "It's not going to be one of these guys."

The others in question all look like they stopped on the way to downtown office jobs. We're about five blocks south of the main office buildings in Dunhare. If we're meeting one of the undercover team, he's not going to be in a suit and tie. A bus squeals to a stop, fumes ghosting in the cold air. A few passengers debark, and an elf breaks into a run, juggling his new foil-wrapped tacos.

I glance across the street. Multiple figures are huddled in sleeping bags or makeshift tents in the deeper alcoves of the building. Police haven't been by yet to gently usher them out and off to whatever street corner they'll take to for the rest of the day. I take warm hands out of my pockets to pay for the brisket and egg combo, and then order a dozen more.

Cieran follows my glance across the street again, and hands over a few bills in exchange for water bottles.

"Hey, Jersey!" The guy behind the truck counter leans forward to greet the scruffy looking guy coming up. Cieran tilts his head and we take a few steps away, hands back in pockets like we're just waiting.

"Jersey" is most likely a human from his taller stature, but it's hard to tell around the dark grey beanie and leather jacket with the collar popped against the cold. Jeans and boots complete it. He slouches as he banters with the food truck guy, but there's something else about him announcing "don't mess with me."

He's our guy.

"Nah, I'm serious. No charge." Food truck guy spreads his hands.

Jersey points at him. "You're the best." If his nickname hadn't already told us, his accent definitely declares eastern Allied States. He pivots, makes us, and then, "Eh, you're kidding me." He strides over, arms wide, locked on Cieran. No hug, they just go for the handshake and shoulder bump. "What are you doing over here, man?"

"Best breakfast in the city," Cieran responds.

Jersey presses a hand to his chest. "You know it."

"Hey, man." He reaches out to me, and I return the greeting. No names.

But now that he's up close, I place him. Specialist Tommy Corsetti, an air warlock who's been with the Guard for two years, mostly with the deep cover division. Always full of advice from his Nona, and has the most ridiculous competition going with Remy on who can cook better food from the worst ration packs.

Remy's winning.

There's a slight tilt to the chin, relief in his eyes to see us, a bit of home and the Guard reaching out through whatever he's wading through on his team's mission.

"How's the girlfriend?" Cieran asks.

"Oh, she's great. You wanna see a picture?" He's already pulling out his phone.

"Of course I do. Gotta make sure she's real." Cieran laughs.

Tommy jostles his shoulder, and they shift to stand out of the reaching sun. I angle myself to keep them blocked from most view and to keep eyes out while Tommy shows pictures of the "girlfriend."

Their voices lower as Tommy skims through pictures, but his accent doesn't really falter, just becomes less broad.

"Was over there as soon as I could get away. By about eighteen fifty. No one in or out until after zero hundred. Then..." Silence falls, broken by a low curse from Cieran. "That your guy?"

"Sure is. Can you send it to Bes?"

"Yeah, got some video too. You know these guys?"

"No, must be some new meatheads he's picked up."

"They're not local," Tommy says. "Here."

A glance from the corner of my eye shows him handing the phone to Cieran, who taps something in. Must be my number since seconds later, my phone hums in my pocket.

"I didn't get much from Ylan. We need to be on the lookout for something?" Tommy glances between us, worry lurking around his eyes.

"Maybe. I don't want to screw with whatever you guys have got going on, but that's one of Andrej's guys. We're not sure who else is in town with him."

"Shit." Tommy rubs his chin. "He coming after you?"

"Might be." Cieran shrugs. "Unless him coming right into the same café as all of us yesterday, and Bes picking him up on cameras within a few blocks of me over the last few weeks is a coincidence."

"You know what we say about coincidence." A faint grin stirs Tommy's face, and we both chuckle. Wolfe's saying has infiltrated pretty much every level of the Guard. Maybe it's not even his and he got it from someone else.

"Thanks for this," Cieran says.

"Anytime," Tommy returns.

"Stay safe out here, Tommy." Cieran claps his shoulder.

Tommy's grin comes tight. "Always." He glances to me. "Tell Rem I'm still gonna kick his ass one of these days, and he better watch out."

I chuckle. "Will do. How much longer you have?"

His hands find his pockets. "Ylan's thinking about another month. Hope to Fates he's right."

"You okay?" It slips out.

Tommy lifts a shoulder. "It's another day, sun's out, breakfast is on the way. So it'll be okay, right?"

Cieran's smile has no humor, just understanding. My fingers brush a medal alongside the rosary and I pull it out, handing it over. Tommy takes it, spinning it and looking at the relief of St. George, dragon slayer.

I've always figured he's as good as any for a patron of the Drax Guard. I've got another medal on the chain with my ident tags.

Tommy's silent for a second, then he lifts it slightly between us. "My Nona's always going on about him. So if Mom's handing it out, must be a good one, huh?"

I roll my eyes at the nickname, but Cieran chuckles.

Tommy tucks the medal into his pocket along with his hands. "Thanks," he tells me.

I nod. "Take care."

"Always." And the carelessness comes back with a thickening to his accent. One more tilt of the chin, then he's striding away, a certain swagger coming back as he takes his food and calls one last farewell to the food truck worker and heads down the street.

Our orders are up next, and we stick our tacos in pockets before carrying the rest across the street. Most of the homeless are awake and still burrowed against the cold. They gratefully take the hot food and clean water.

"You know St. John's has an overnight shelter," I tell a young human mom who's got a small kid tucked up against her. And a program to help single moms get back on their feet.

"It was full up last night," an elf with age lines starting around his eyes replies. "Don't worry. We're taking care of them."

The mom flashes a smile at the speaker. Despite the street, she and the kid are neat and as clean as they can be. "We'll be okay. We've managed so far."

I offer another smile and tuck another twenty in with the tacos I hand her. "Managing." That seems like the worst word. Not going up or down, just staying where you are, keeping head above water, but no sign of rescue.

"Take care."

She smiles and the kid eagerly unwraps the taco. I back away a few steps, waiting on Cieran who's talking with a white-haired guy, one who's wearing an old Army cover. Some aging veteran who couldn't quite get back into society or lost his benefits, I don't know.

But it has the lump growing in my chest again. Maybe he just couldn't figure out how to deal with some injury and still wakes up sweating in the middle of the night.

Though I've got a huge family who'll drag me home to at least sleep on couches long before I end up roaming the streets. And that creates another pressure bubble. Maybe this guy lost everyone and he doesn't have anyone else.

My phone buzzes, and I fish it out. Unknown number. I start to dismiss it until I see the three missed calls from Nadire alongside the messages from Tommy.

I answer.

"Hi! Is this Besim?" The woman's voice sounds vaguely familiar, and at my cautious "yes" she goes on. "This is Maya, I work at Nadire's café. Um, she gave me your number to call."

I can definitely *hear* my sister in the background. Her high-pitched words are too fast to pick out any details.

"She's on the phone with the police right now."

"She's *what*?"

"We're okay," Maya hastily reassures. "She wanted me to ask you to get over here as fast as you could, please? She said a lot of other things, but that's the gist of it." Apology takes over.

"I can be there in about ten minutes."

"Okay." Maya exhales in quick relief. "I'll let her know."

Cieran taps my arm, question in his eyes as he tips a nod at the phone. I lift my hand slightly, reassuring. I think.

"Do you need me to stay on the phone?" I ask.

"You can if you want to get yelled at for not answering your phone." I can hear Maya's sympathetic wince accompanying her words. I pinch the bridge of my nose. Telling Nadire I didn't hear or feel the call won't go over well at all.

"But you two are okay?"

"Yes."

"Okay, we'll be there as fast as we can."

"Thanks." And she hangs up.

"What's going on?" Cieran's question gets put on pause as I skim through the missed calls one after another, and one text message that's
-*PICK UP YOUR PHONE.*-

"Something happened at Nadi's shop and she asked if I'd come over." I show him the message and he winces for me. "You want to come watch me get yelled at by my little sister?"

Cieran chuckles. "Sure." He inclines his head at the old veteran. "We've also got some more boots on the ground in case our friend shows up."

The old guy catches my glance and salutes. I acknowledge and then Cieran and I are off, catching a bus to get us halfway, and then walking the rest.

And once we round the corner and get a view of the coffee shop from across the street, we break into a run.

7

BESIM

Swirling red graffiti covers the bricked front of the café, slashing through the *Fox and Ground* window logo, shimmering as the sun slices down the street on its continued rise.

Nadire stands outside, arms waving and voice raised at some uniformed officer just trying to write something on his tablet, perhaps having given up trying to get a word in edgewise. Maya is a few steps away, biting at her thumb, switching her attention between Nadire, the graffiti, and the street.

She brightens substantially when she sees us and waves us over like we're not already hustling.

"What happened?" Cieran beats me to it.

"It was here this morning," Maya says. "Neither of us knew since we come in the back and the window shades were down. The logo usually casts some funky shadows on the ground with the shades down anyway. It wasn't until we noticed people hurrying by that we thought anything of it. Then one of our regulars came in and told us and…" Her hands wave toward Nadire.

"This looks like some sort of warning or threat runes." Cieran studies the lines, then lifts a shoulder. Like me, he's not very fluent in the runic language of magic since we have none to harness or cast. We'll need Remy.

"Finally." Nadire stomps over, throwing one last glare over her shoulder at the policeman who just turns and leaves with a very efficient walk.

She's scowling and if steam started coming from her ears, I wouldn't be surprised. "He said there's nothing to be done since we didn't see anything. They'll have someone patrol down here more regularly just in case. And I'm going to have to pay for at least a warlock from city cleaning to come out since the asshole who did this used magic."

"Don't bother with that. I'll call Rem," I say.

"Are you sure he'll *answer his phone*?" She glares at me.

"Nadi." My head tilts slightly as I try to keep hold of the anger that's so quick to rise up these days. "I was working."

"Working?" She scoffs. "It's not even seven-thirty. Don't try to pretend you weren't still asleep and were ghosting me."

"Nadi." My tone cuts sharp. Her glare doesn't let up and I tilt my head at Cieran, hoping she puts it together that I'm here within ten minutes of Maya's call with my potential sergeant instead of the twenty it'd take from the house.

"Did you see anything happen?" Cieran butts in, saving us both from continuing to poke each other.

Nadi pointedly turns to him, physically placing her shoulder to me. I roll my eyes and focus my attention up and down the street. Nothing, no cameras around. But I'd need Rem or Dejan to tell me if there's any magical wards or watchers for the other businesses.

Nadire denies seeing anything, but Cieran keeps calm. He still has dark circles under his eyes, probably hasn't slept all week, but looks way more alert and energetic than he did at this same spot yesterday.

"Okay, you have any cameras inside?"

Nadi makes sure to squint another glare at me when she answers. "I actually do."

Cieran's brow arches, but he's wise enough not to comment. "Okay, Besim, go see if there's anything. Check yesterday too."

He's already beat me to it, and I feel stupid for not having thought to come back by for the camera yesterday to see where Janvier went or how long he hung around after we left.

"I'll call Rem," Cieran says. "Nadire, right?" He smiles and Nadire appears charmed. She's going to be devastated when she finds out he's already claimed by a dragonwalker. "Why don't you hang with me out here and we can wait for Remy."

"That's a great idea." She sends one more glare toward me that I ignore in favor of going inside.

There aren't many customers inside, most probably having been scared off by the graffiti or possibly the yelling shop owner outside.

"Do you know where you're looking?" Maya's voice has me jolting. I hadn't heard her follow me.

I manage to recover somewhat gracefully and *not* almost punch her in the face. "Yeah."

"Okay." She's fiddling with her apron strings. "Can I get you guys anything?"

"Cieran will probably take a coffee."

Maya arches one eyebrow slightly. "But what do *you* need?"

It takes me off guard again, like she's asking a deeper question than *do you need a drink of the non-alcoholic variety?*

"I'm good."

Okay, great. Even strangers are giving me that look of *sure.*

I head away from it into the back office, pulling out my laptop and hooking it to the computer to download the recent security footage. I'm pulling the last few months just to be safe, because patterns don't start in twenty-four hours.

Once it's transferred over to my laptop, I take it back out. Unlike yesterday, there's something about the smaller office and its light grey walls feeling like it's looming over me, compressing against my frame.

At least out in the open café, I don't feel like I'm about to have some sort of panic attack.

Most of the tables are still empty, all sized slightly differently to make elves, fae, humans, dwarves, and really tall trolls comfortable. Nadire did think that one through. The high-top I prefer is taken, so I just set the laptop down on the open end of the stainless-steel counter, my back to the wall. I don't really need this out in the open where anyone can look over my shoulder and wonder why I'm scrolling security footage.

"Oh. Sorry." Maya comes back over and scoots some thick textbooks and notebooks down to give me more room. Block print titles jump out—*Architecture, Middle Centuries Art History, Basics of Non-Magic Engineering.*

"Yours?" I tilt a nod. Stupid, because I know Nadi's not studying that stuff.

"Yeah. I'm going for Architecture. Year two." She tucks hands in her back pockets, shrugging a shoulder like it's not a big deal.

I drag a stool up. "Enjoying it so far?"

A grin splits her face and I'm staring as suddenly I'm taking in more details about her. Pale blue shirt and distressed jeans, a warmth to her black skin as the sunlight rebounds off the counter. Tiny butterfly clips are tucked into her natural curls, pinning it back from her face and showing the pointed tips to her ears. Eyes are dark, but that same renegade sunlight is showing the layered shades of brown beneath the grey ring announcing her fae parentage.

"Yeah, it's been so fun! This semester is harder with more specific classes. I don't know, maybe it's just finally getting to do this after a few years of dreaming about it, but it hasn't worn off yet."

The joy radiating off her draws a smile from me. "Maybe you can pass some of that excitement to our younger brother. He's complaining his way through his degree."

She laughs, and it seems like the butterflies in her hair twitch and brighten with the sound. Might be magic, since all half-fae have it thanks to the strength of fae genes that dominate everything. Or maybe I should just stop staring.

"How old is he?"

"Nineteen," I reply and cue up the screens, starting back at the beginning of the footage I downloaded.

"Ah. I already did the growing up and now I'm a super serious adult going back to school with all the kids. I'm not really into the partying or skipping classes to hang out on the quad thing."

"You move here for school?" I glance her way, and then try to focus back on the footage now playing. It's a decent view from the corner just above my head. It's going to be pretty boring watching people in and out and sitting at tables working on laptops, so I bump up the speed.

"Sort of." She moves off down the counter, steaming milk and grabbing some flavor syrup to dump into a cup. "My brother is a mess and I'm done with all the stuff he's into, so I got as far from it as I could and thought I'd finally get to school too."

"You keeping in contact at all?" I make sure my program for spotting Janvier is also keyed into the footage, that way I don't have to try to watch for him and any other potential suspects.

"Nope." Something clatters firmly to the counter and I glance up. Her lips press in a thin line, and she's really focused on the drink in front of her.

"Sorry." I wince slightly.

She inhales and straightens her shoulders, turning back to me, grabbing a lid as she comes and snugging it on.

"It's okay. I'll admit I'm a little jealous when Nadi talks about all you guys and how close you all seem. Here." She hands me the cup. I'm not sure what I'm more taken aback by—Nadi talking about us nonstop, or the drink being offered.

Maya hesitates, seeming unsure all of the sudden. "You never technically said yes *or* no to the drink, and you look like you need something, so..." She holds it out further and I finally take it.

"Thanks. Though you might not want to tell your boss you're making free coffee for the brother she's mad at."

"I can charge you if that makes you feel better?" Maya lifts her shoulders and it brings a chuckle from me.

"Maybe. What is it?"

"Well, I remember hearing yesterday how much you love peppermint."

I freeze and she laughs, freeing me from the sudden awkwardness of having to drink something I hate.

"No, it's the same drink Nadi sprang on you yesterday. You didn't seem to hate it, so hope that's okay."

I set it on the counter, opting to let it cool for a second before scalding my mouth. "Yeah, that was really good. Your recipe, right?"

She sticks hands in her back pockets again, boot scuffing against the ground. "I don't know that I'm taking *all* the credit. It's a riff on a drink I loved to get at my favorite coffee shop back in Detroit. And now I know how to do all this, figured I'd give it a shot."

"You should count it as a success." I lift the cup in brief salute and drink.

"Thanks." Her smile returns and maybe it's the morning continuing to flood the café that makes things seem brighter.

A backpack sits on the floor, and a pin on the front pocket catches my eye as I set the coffee down. Three stars triangulated over three slashing blue lines. Given its vicinity to the textbooks and the pin, it's definitely not Nadi's. I flick a look at Maya where she leans against the counter.

"*Starfall* fan?" I ask.

Another smile lights up her face. "Huge," she admits and crosses over to nudge the backpack enough to show a commander badge nestled in among some other buttons and decorative pins. "It's kind of kept me sane for the last few years."

"I know the feeling." There's been more than one mission I've come home from and finally fallen asleep to episodes replaying on my laptop in the late night or early morning. "You seen all the shows?" I glance back at the security footage in front of me.

"Yep. Multiple times. And the original movie."

The movie is over ten years old and not that great, but the more dedicated fans still love it. I glance back. "Game?"

She chuckles and the clips in her hair flutter wings again. "I've logged probably a depressing amount of hours on it. Beat it twice."

I take another drink and refocus on the laptop. "Three times for me."

"Showoff." Maya huffs in mock-disgust.

A smile escapes me. "I haven't played in awhile. Last time tried a darkpath run, but didn't make it far."

Maya laughs as she reaches over the counter to take the ceramic mug an elf in a ratty beanie is returning. His dark shirt has a purposefully faded image of a nineteenth century Caesar, the last before the Empire fell, who thought he was something of a philosopher like his early forebears. The elf is not a threat.

"I tried once and chickened out one session in," she admits and it takes a second to come back to *Starfall* and not threat assessment. Our reasons for abandoning that gameplay version are probably wildly different. Unlikely she was getting flashbacks to a joint allies mission in South America to take out a drug cartel.

"I'd be suspicious if you made it all the way through," I say, and she makes a wry face of agreement.

"I'd be worried about me too." She moves away to take another order. Anyone she's helped so far goes away infinitely more relaxed after a few minutes' interaction at the register. I snag my cup again, admitting that it's working on me too. I feel much more at ease than when I sat down.

Movement outside the window announces Remy's arrival. He stares at the graffiti, a frown twisting his face. Nadi's arms are crossed over her stomach, and she's not even trying to flirt with him. Worry shrouds her stance next to Cieran whose hands are in his pockets.

Someone stops and Nadi forces a smile and waves them in. The customer slides in past Remy who's calling up some of his magic. Deep blue, the hottest part of a fire, grabs my eyes. The way it flickers and dances up his wrists before he raises a hand to target the graffiti has my pulse racing faster. A buzzing builds up in my ears and, even though I'm sitting in a café miles from the Wastelands, I feel like I'm about to fall into some hole like the ones that'll open without warning out there.

"You okay?"

I jerk, almost spilling the coffee I'm clutching in one hand. Maya stands next to me, having apparently taken and fulfilled the order of whoever stepped inside. I quickly set the cup down and turn back to the laptop.

"Yeah." I clear my throat and try to actually pay attention to what's in front of me as she grabs a towel and bottle and goes to clean a newly vacated table and chat with some other customers.

It takes five minutes before I see something and it's not what I expected. I slow things down and watch Cieran come in with a woman. She's moving slowly and he looks about the same as he does now. Terrible.

I check the time stamp. Three months ago. My stomach does a flip, same as it did yesterday when I looked at another ghost on this same screen.

I'm watching him and his sister come in, order coffee and some pastries. Nadi smiling at them. Cieran helping his sister get comfortable in a chair and grabbing their orders. Them sitting and laughing, soaking up the sunlight and being alive for a little longer. This would have been just weeks before she passed.

He's still outside in the present, watching Remy work, frown pressing his face into seriousness.

A lot of other Guard had been trying to check on him, but he kept his phone shut off most days before our deployment. I didn't know him very well before, and then I think I just annoyed him into having a slight breakdown in the middle of the mission.

I slam the key harder than needed to speed up the video again. Still nothing. Nothing lurking outside the view I get of the window overnight or in the early morning hours that speed by. Cieran comes by once more, alone this time, grabbing a coffee and sitting at the same table for a few minutes before leaving.

Maya stays nearby, but she doesn't make a move to restart our conversation. Maybe because I'm glaring at the laptop, kicked back to the clawing unease, and I'm not sure how to shake it again.

Nothing and nothing. Until I get to yesterday. By now the others have come in, Remy reassuring Nadi that the graffiti is gone and is nothing to worry about. But he holds something in his hand—a small containment glass. He found something in the graffiti, but isn't saying anything in front of the two women. From Cieran's brief tilt of the head, he had been right about the runes.

Unease stirs. This is a safe part of town. It being a random occurrence reeks of coincidence, and it's really unflattering what Wolfe says about that. If Janvier is targeting Cieran, why did he or one of his guys tag my sister's coffee shop?

Nadi still ignores me, and now takes the opportunity to try to coax something more from Remy as she makes tea in thanks since he's refusing any payment.

But I'm locked on to the screen, not even acknowledging Cieran coming around to look over my shoulder.

In the footage, Janvier walks into the shop. Sits close to our table. We leave. And minutes later he comes up to the counter, chats amiably with Nadi and Maya, shakes her hand, shoots one look at the camera, and leaves.

I hit pause and swivel the computer to face her as she comes over to hand the tea to Remy.

"What did this guy talk to you about?"

Nadi draws back, shoulders braced, and chin tipped up like she's ready to fight. "Uh, we just talked, Besim. Is that a crime now?"

"It is when he's a terrorist."

She scoffs, crossing her arms tight over her chest. "A terrorist? Please. Is that all guys who flirt with your sister and are complimentary of their business?"

"Nadi..." I warn, knowing I need to get a grip and try not to shout this to the entire shop, but something's got its claws under my skin and is tugging. Pulling until the deep rage that I guess I've been suppressing all my life is going to come out.

"Commiserating over brothers in the Army, okay?" Thankfully she must read it's really not the morning for a sibling spat.

"*Ancrit*," Cieran mutters under his breath, keeping the curse in elvish—vaguely more polite for the women's sake.

I might agree since I don't remember anything about Janvier having brothers or being linked to the Armed Forces in any way. But I've been missing things all over the place.

"Then what?" I ask.

"It's not the morning for twenty questions about the random guy, Bes," she says through gritted teeth, shooting a glance at my crew.

"Humor me," I return in much the same tone.

"We introduced ourselves, shook hands like you can *see in the video*, had a quick makeout session and he's coming over as my new husband tomorrow night."

"Nadi." Saints help me.

"Literally whatever happened in the video is what happened, Bes." She props her hands against her hips and looks scarily like Mom.

"He shook your hand?" Remy butts in suddenly.

Nadi blushes and looks to him.

"Let me see?"

Okay, what the hell?

Now my crewmate is holding my sister's hand, and the idiot is about to make her infatuation with him worse. But he frowns, and pulls his thumb across her palm. I don't smash the heel of my hand against my forehead, though I really want to. Her face is beet red as he releases her hand and takes a step back like he's trying to avoid getting caught up in the awkward explosion he's about to cause.

"Sorry, your brother's paranoia rubbed off on me." His hand curls up like he's holding something else.

Okay, that was a smooth attempt at flirting. Except for the look he darts at us and the way he edges farther from her like he'd now prefer to be halfway across the country. And the way he's never flirted with anyone before. I know he's not pining after her the way she is for him.

Cieran coughs and accepts the cup Maya hands him. Maya's got much of our skepticism in her eyes as she takes in all four of us.

I close the laptop and sweep it into my backpack. "If this guy comes back in, I want you to call me immediately."

Nadi crosses her arms again, rubbing her palms against her upper arms, *not* looking at Remy. "What if you don't answer your phone again?"

We're still on that apparently.

"Then Cieran's going to give you his number and *you're going to call the sergeant.*"

Nadi rolls her eyes. "Okay, *fine.*"

I shove to my feet, leaving Cieran and Remy behind, needing air and to get out before *I'm* the one to cause an Antilles clan war.

8

NADIRE

WE'RE ALL STARING AFTER Besim as he practically storms out. Remy's already moving, which is good because the moment where he was holding my hand turned out to be unbelievably awkward. I'm not sure I can ever look him in the eye again.

Maya extends a pen and pad of paper to Cieran. He scrawls out his number and hands the paper back. "You both keep this number around. We're serious. Call if you see him again."

I want to make some sort of smart comment, but my arms are crossed, hands tucked against my sides. Grim seriousness weighs around the sergeant. And something is wrong with Besim.

"Okay." It comes hushed from me. Even the other customers don't seem to stir until the bell announces Cieran's departure.

"What the hell?" Maya bumps my arm with her elbow and it loosens my limbs enough for me to scrub my palms against each other.

That slight brush of Remy's finger against my skin still lingers. You'd think that would have been the thing to really send me over the edge on this crush, but instead it might have punted me into a completely different sort of disarray.

I've never experienced the "skin-crawling" feeling until the brush of his thumb. And not because he's suddenly weird. It's because it felt like he was *scraping something off*.

I scrub my hands harder against each other. At least the headache that's stuck around since yesterday despite the pain meds finally decides to take off.

"Nadi." Maya gently touches my wrists and a bit of calm floods in. Fast enough for me to manage a frown.

"Did you just use magic on me?"

Her answering smile isn't even sorry. "Yeah. You looked like you were about to go full Lady Macbeth."

"Oh no." I force my hands apart. "Are you a nerd too?"

"Hardly. It's Shakespeare and everyone saw the movie last year." She arches her eyebrow as my hands creep toward each other again.

I check the café. If the three people noticed how unusual the last few minutes were with all of us clustered around the counter and then the guys abruptly leaving, they're being really nice and not staring. All the same, I keep my voice really low. She's half-fae, she'll be able to hear just fine.

"There hasn't been anything weird in the news recently, right?"

Maya leans against the counter next to me. "You're asking the college student who lives either on campus or here?"

"I forgot you have no life." I force a grin.

She bumps my arm again, mock offense in her gasp. "What kind of weird?"

"Like..." My shoulders lift as I tuck my arms across my stomach again. "Like a few years ago when that guy was setting off magic traps and bombs in city parks and buildings and stuff."

Terrorist sticks in my throat. That's what they called the guy from yesterday. Even if I really don't want to know *exactly* what it is they do in the Drax Guard, I know there was a team after that asshole a few years ago. And Besim and his team are on this elf now.

If that's what he really is. He seemed nice and friendly. But terrorists were shadowy figures who lived in far-away countries torn apart by war and unrest. Right?

It makes me curl more into myself. Guess this is just another way I'm naïve and blissfully unaware of actions and consequences. Just like half the family probably thinks.

"I think even I'd hear about it if there was," Maya says before moving to the register to help a new customer. Hopefully it'll pick up now there's no magical graffiti all over the front of the café.

"Though I did hear the sergeant say the graffiti looked like a threat or warning." She winces as she says it, maybe regretting saying it as my blood pressure spikes again.

"Do you know if it was?" I manage to ask. She's got magic, and I don't, and I barely paid attention in fourth grade magic basics.

She shakes her head. "Fae and half-fae don't need runes to cast. And I didn't really get anything more than casting basics in high school to use mine." Her lips clamp shut after that.

Usually parents, or mentors in a trade school are the ones to teach more than public school basics. It doesn't sound like she had either of those things to teach more Gaelic High Fae language to help her use the wild magic pooling in natural reservoirs or humming through the air. A tug comes at my heart, and I guess I really am an Antilles the way I want to drag her home and introduce her to family in all its chaotic mess and glory.

She turns to help the next customer. I twist my hair up into a crappy bun to preemptively stop myself from tugging it into knots when I inevitably start to overthink or stress about anything that's happened in the last twenty-four hours.

Order comes down for a toffee-nut latte with an extra pump of caramel. I grab a cup and start working, wondering if I'm always going to be pulling shifts at my own coffee shop, taking a smaller compensation home so I can keep paying employees like Maya. All while the knots in my shoulders cinch tighter every day as I keep trying to figure out how to make it.

That quiet voice in the back of my mind reminds me I can ask literally anyone in the family for help. Even if that's just advice. But I'm never asking for anything remotely financial, especially from Dad.

I shove the thought back down as I replace the portafilter on the espresso machine and go for the milk next. I'm going to make this work by myself.

Maya chats with the customer as she heats up the cranberry scone that completes the order. I should ask my sister Elsie if she wants to join forces to provide baked goods for the shop, help get her dreams of a small baking business off the ground. She did some for me when I was getting started, but then we argued about something stupid, and she got busy with culinary school, and now I buy wholesale from another business.

I'd need to prove this is turning into a viable business before approaching her again, because she'll ask all the questions, want to see the books, ask financial terms I'm still learning and don't want to get explained from Astrid in her amazing business casual clothes.

The milk carafe clatters back into place with my overly aggressive slam. Maybe I got all the troll traits that Besim didn't, and I can add quick anger to the list of things which set me apart. Guess I never got the anger management lessons some of the rest of the siblings did.

I press the lid onto the paper cup, but it's stubbornly refusing to slide over the lip on one side. I'm gathering one deep breath to more carefully place it before I spill coffee everywhere, when an explosion rocks the café.

9

BESIM

"BES!" REMY CALLS AS my boots hit the sidewalk opposite the café. My shoulders rise, but I'm not so far stuck in my own head to keep walking and then really make them concerned or mad. So I stop.

He jogs across the street, hand still curled around something as he joins me.

"You trying to make things weird with my sister?" I manage to ask, the accompanying smile awkwardly straining my face.

Remy winces. "Yeah, sorry if I did." He shuffles back a step, like he might be worried about my reaction. "It wasn't until she said he shook her hand that I was able to pinpoint what I was sensing in there."

"What was it?" I lean closer and I feel the burst of heat from his clenched hand—thankfully no light to remind me of fire—and his jaw tenses as he shakes his head.

"Feels like a low-level mind reading charm."

"It's a *what*?" I lurch forward a step. Wasn't bad enough that Janvier was stalking us, but he tried to skim information from my sister?

Remy's fist knocks my chest, barely calming me from...doing what, I'm not sure.

"I'll have to try to pull it apart to see if or what information he got from her. But—" he taps his jacket pocket—"got some other stuff from the graffiti to look at in the lab."

Motion brings Cieran to our side.

"You get something?" he asks Remy without stopping. We hurry to join.

"Those were warning runes," Remy replies. "Definitely making a threat, but not sure against who." He flicks a glance at me, and it seems he's thinking the same thing. If Janvier is after Cieran, why did the *Fox and Ground* get tagged?

"I pulled some trace magic off it, but I'll need to get it to the tower and run a few tests to see if it's Janvier's."

"Go ahead. Bes and I will be right behind you." Cieran pulls out his phone and sends a quick text. "Dejan's covering our six right now, but he'll shadow you, Rem. The tagging was fresh."

I don't look behind us for the elf, but I feel immediately calmer knowing he's somewhere out there.

Remy nods. "Cameras pick up anything?"

I flash back to the images of Cieran and his sister, but that's not important right now. He might not even want to see something like that. But Remy's asking about actual security.

"No, not besides Janvier in the café yesterday."

"It's a hell of a coincidence her place got targeted, especially if she let slip that you're military." Cieran's not judging, at least externally. But it's hard not to take it personally when it's my own sister who just exposed all of us and herself as a target.

"If he's following same operations as last time, there's probably something left in the spell I got off the walls," Remy says.

"Most likely. Head off and see if you can get a head start on it."

Remy's barely three steps ahead when he slams to a halt, twisting to his left and the open street, flinging up a hand. His magic crackles to life, but it's not enough to stop what I'm finally hearing.

A keening whistle, then impact, all within milliseconds.

Bright light floods my vision, followed by thunder, and then I'm weightless and falling.

10

BESIM

MY BACK HITS THE sidewalk, breath rushing out and sky fuzzing above me for a second. Sound blurs and is eclipsed by a sharp ringing in my ears. The shock isn't enough to stop me craning my head up, trying to move, check myself and the others.

Dust billows in front of me, held back by Remy's humming, blue-tinted shield. His feet skid backward as something pushes hard against it. He opens his right hand and slams it into place against the barrier, dropping something small that shatters on the ground. The shield strengthens.

My boots scrape the sidewalk as I try to get up, pain shooting through my back and down my leg. I ignore it, still focused on Remy until a sound yanks my attention left.

Cieran's a tangled mess against the wall, limbs jerking to shield his head from masonry tumbling out of the impact site above him.

"Sarge!" Remy shouts, trying to get a look over his shoulder.

"I got him, Rem!" Dejan tears up the sidewalk behind us, meeting my gaze before sliding to his knees by Cieran.

Remy speaks some counter-ward in Hawaiian, then he spreads his hands and the shield curls forward, wrapping around something, compressing, and smothering it into nothing.

Shouts and screams start to break through the ringing, and I jerk a look around. Civilians are running, some staring in shock at Remy or the mess behind him, the cars that wrecked as drivers swerved in surprise or maybe got hit in the crossfire.

Get up, my head is telling me, and I start to obey, shrugging out of the backpack before the sight of blood on my hand halts me. Bleeding from somewhere. My stoneskin should have kicked in automatically at any hint of threat. Should have emerged when I started falling. But it *didn't.*

"Bes!" Remy's voice jerks my head up. He reaches out, deep blue magic still flickering around his wrists, wicking around his jacket sleeves.

I scramble away from the sight, some sound catching in my throat, until my back slams against the wall, sending the pain shooting again.

"Bes, hey!" The fire dies and his hands clench into my jacket. I grab his wrists, skin against skin, my body's protective armor still not activating. That makes me try to hurl him away.

But he's planted, and I can't shift him. Or I lost every bit of strength I ever had in the explosion.

"Besim!" He shakes me and my head wobbles enough to snap me into focus. A sharp breath rushes from me and he leans back, hauling me up. "You with me?"

Remy has to push against my chest again, keeping me from folding forward once I'm on my feet, that shattered feeling rushing all around me. But I'm still in one piece. I think.

"Yeah." My voice is hoarse.

"Okay, we've got to pinpoint the source." He turns to the street, chaos still reigning.

Dejan has Cieran sitting up against the wall, covered in dust and hat knocked off.

"I'm *fine*!" Cieran shouts as Dejan holds him in place, trying to assess for injury. Cieran slams a hand against his forehead, wincing as he repeats the reassurance. He's not talking to Dejan.

"Hey, warlock!" A new voice cuts across the noise.

Janvier. He stands across the street, smirking at us and the destruction he caused. Remy and I both start toward him, Remy in the lead to maintain a magical barrier.

But Janvier turns away and waves his hand. The buildings behind him shudder, and glass, brick, and rebar rip from the structure, threatening the civilians all along the sidewalk and the ones still in their cars.

Expletives drop and Remy lunges forward, spreading his hands as his counter-magic flies out, catching what he can all at once, a few smaller bits smashing into falling rock before it can hit someone.

"Bes!" he grits out, hitting his knees, trying to hold it all. But he didn't have time to center and set. We'll need to move fast before he drains his magic. Screams and confusion ricochet as people try to get away. In the midst of it, Janvier meets my gaze, a bit of triumph shining through pure rage. Bright purple threaded with black coils about his hand, and he thrusts his arm out, shooting stolen magic right at me.

Remy's shout is lost in the humming panic of magic coming right at me without the comforting rush of my stoneskin emerging to protect me from all but burning wildfire.

"Bes!" Cieran appears, shield whipping up in front of us, his shoulder driving into my chest as the spell hits the ward-reinforced surface of his shield and shoves us both over. The same stabbing through my back now has a partner where Cieran's solid frame landed on my chest. Wailing sirens join the ringing in my ears.

My head cranes up and I meet Janvier's fury before the sorcerer points at me in silent promise and then vanishes.

Cieran struggles to his feet, cursing in two different languages, stumbling forward to help Dejan get people off the street as Remy strains to hold the debris. I stagger up from the ground, but Janvier is gone.

Remy curses again, but I ignore him, trusting him to keep his counter-measures up as long as he can while I help get people out of the destructive path before he has to drop it all.

Thankfully there's a few other men and women who react like us and start shepherding others across the street, still darting fearful glances above them at the suspended debris.

Once everyone is clear, Remy starts trying to lower it, but something *snaps* as it's halfway, and the remains crash to the sidewalk, more dust and surprised shouts erupting. He pitches onto his hands, one elbow buckling and sending his face dangerously close to the asphalt.

I lurch forward. Somewhere in the last minutes the pain has reduced, but my hearing hasn't quite snapped back to normal. I get an arm underneath him and practically pick him up. He leans heavily on me as we stagger back to the sidewalk and he collapses onto the curb.

Dejan instantly appears, one hand on Remy's forehead, bringing his head up, checking pupils and response. Remy blinks slowly, not focused.

"You have any on you?" Dejan asks.

"No." Remy slurs the word.

It was too quick, too big a burst of magic without proper preparation in what he did that left him temporarily drained, system overloaded. If he hadn't stopped in time, he might have used up all his magic and ended up in a coma.

"I told you to stop letting Bear eat your emergency stash." Dejan digs in the inside chest pocket of his jacket and pulls out a small foil-wrapped piece of chocolate. Backup stash for when Remy's three-year-old son inevitably squirrels or cajoles his away.

"He keeps sneaking it." Remy tips forward and Dejan catches him shoulder to shoulder as he unwraps the chocolate and puts it in Remy's hand. The warlock manages to get it in his mouth, face contorting around the sweetness he dislikes before he starts chewing.

Once he's safely leaning on his knees, head hanging low as whatever is in the chocolate helps kickstart magic recovery, Dejan rises back to his feet.

"You okay?" he asks me.

Cop cars screech around the corner, officers piling out to start assessing the scene. Fire trucks aren't far behind, fire and water warlocks and a few other magic users on the crews ready to suppress fire or any other lingering magic.

"Yeah. Maybe." I lift my bleeding hand.

"Shit, Bes!" He jerks forward, snagging my arm. Cieran slowly limps over as a stinging feeling rushes over my skin. Dejan's elven magic, trained for healing, seeking out injury.

It brings back a vague memory—Rem leaned over me, blocking out the Wastelands skies, fire engulfing him without hurting as he tries to get the wild magic off me as it burns and *burns* into my skin. Dejan appearing, and the same intense burst hitting my skin, trying to salvage what it could before needing someone with more skill to keep healing.

I jerk away, feet stumbling a step.

"You're okay." Dejan's voice has calming cadence to it—something that's very rare to hear from him, so it should shock me into being still. But something about it has my hackles rising and me backing off again.

"Bes." His normal tone cuts through.

Rem lifts his head and fixes me with a more focused look.

They're both watching me, wary, ready. They know something's wrong, and that might make things worse.

"Let him look at you, Bes," Cieran says. An order. I stick my arm back out and Dejan takes it, more subtle feeling sweeping over me this time. "Remy, you good?"

"Yeah, Sarge."

"That was good work." Cieran stiffly leans down and taps Remy's shoulder. The warlock offers a nod and faint smile back. "Anyone get eyes on?"

"It was Janvier," Remy reports. Dejan's hold tightens around my arm right as a brighter stinging hits my elbow and forearm. I scowl and he glares right back, not apologizing for healing what feels like some pretty thorough gouges from hitting the ground twice.

"I got sidetracked with that stunt he pulled. Bes?" Remy turns it to me.

"Literally vanished," I state. "Didn't see a flash or anything, so not sure what he did."

Remy levers himself up. "I'll go check it."

"Okay, we've got incoming." Cieran jerks his chin at approaching officers. "I'll take point with them. We're still running lead on this. Rem, you and Bes see what you can find."

Another sharp sting and something in my back rights itself. A surprised grunt escapes and I jab out at Dejan. He gracefully avoids it, smug that he got the drop on me and got any potential injury taken care of.

"He good?" Cieran asks and Dejan steps back, flicking his fingers in and out.

"Yeah."

I glare, but he just gives a challenging look back. I ignore it, trying to cover the way I want to move my shoulders, twist a little, to convince my body it's all in one piece.

"Good. See if anyone else needs medical attention."

Dejan salutes and makes his way to the nearest group of paramedics and civilians.

Cieran heads off the officer and suited detective, pulling out his Army ID and staking claim to our case. A news van has arrived, and reporters are descending. I'm still close enough to Dejan to see his irritated expression as they start pushing in and asking questions while he's making sure there's not much more than scrapes and bruises.

A paramedic on scene recognizes him and they fall to chatting amiably while they make their way around. Sometimes it's hard to remember he was a paramedic before he joined the Army and worked his way to the Drax Guard with the rest of us.

"Bes!" Remy's voice cuts across all the chatter and I make my way over to where he stands on the opposite sidewalk, frowning at open air.

"What did you find?" I pick my way around rubble to stand next to him. A glance over my shoulder shows some cameras pointed at us and other survivors watching. "And don't make it flashy," I mutter under my breath.

"Yeah," he says, the same light frustration that people are watching. We tend to try to stay *out* of everyone's sight. "It's a slip-gate." His hand pushes against something invisible. "It's still open."

We exchange a glance. The others are still busy, and even from my limited knowledge, slip-gates don't stay open too long.

"Any way to tell where it goes or how long it might still be here?" I ask, just to make sure.

Remy shakes his head. "Usually only one way to find out. What do you have right now?"

"Three knives." I check my phone, thankfully not broken or cracked from getting caught in the concussive blast of whatever Janvier threw at us. And some way to communicate. "You?"

"Two knives, basalt blade." He waves a hand at his side and the cunningly magic-obscured short sword with basalt inlay he'll use to help focus his power appears. "My magic might be shaky for another few minutes."

"Okay." I whistle a signal and get Cieran's and Dejan's attention again while Remy keeps a hand on the slip-gate. *Checking something out. Comms open,* I sign over to them. Cieran affirms, and I unzip my jacket, drawing one of the knives sheathed against my ribs. I tap Remy's shoulder, resting my fist there and getting ready to follow him through.

"Shield up," he murmurs and this time the sight of his magic flaring is comforting.

"Besim!"

I twist around, the sound of my sister's voice shouting my name distracting me for a second. Nadire runs toward me, shock and relief in her face. Until I turn away and follow Remy through the gate.

11

Besim

A prickle hits my skin as we move through the gate, but still doesn't shift to the protective grey stone barrier. It's only the briefest second before we're through. A faintly burnt smell tinges the open air and four figures spin as soon as an alley solidifies around us. Janvier and three men.

The elf hurls crackling green bolts of magic. Remy grabs the sword buckled to his right hip with the same hand and yanks it out, holding it parallel in front of us. The basalt inlay in the fuller glows red as it reinforces his shielding spell.

A *snick* behind us announces the slip-gate closed forever.

I shift grip on my dirk so the blade points forward. Janvier keeps up the barrage and Remy spreads his left hand wider, blue deepening around his skin as he calls up a stronger ward. The three other men with Janvier flank him, pulling out swords or daggers, their shapes flickering through the magic spearing between us.

"Rem?" I ask, keeping one hand settled on his shoulder.

"Ready," he grunts back, and I shift my feet, ready to push forward. "Go."

He stomps one foot and twists to his left, redirecting the oncoming attack, and sending it back at Janvier and the stocky half-fae next to him.

I push around Remy's right side, coming at the other men who paused for a moment, maybe surprised Janvier can be beaten at the magic game.

The wiry human swipes out with his knife, stance horribly off. All it takes is a slight lean to move around the attack, a grab of his wrist and I slam the hilt of my dirk against his beanie-covered head. He collapses and the second, another human with a scarred cheek leaps back a step, sword between us. No magic or I'd have gotten hit with something by now.

The clash of steel announces Remy engaging and the burning smell intensifies. Remy's magic has a crisp, clean scent to it, and this is slightly left of sour. The swordwielder comes at me, lunging and swinging. I retreat, steadily dodging. I reverse my grip on the dirk again, using it to help reinforce my forearm as I get an arm up and block the overhead chop coming my way.

Stinging erupts through my forearm and I almost curse. My stoneskin is still not appearing, and I don't have my bracer or chain mail on either, pulling this move like an absolute idiot.

But I push my arm up higher, getting some better leverage to sweep my arm out in an arc, knocking him off-balance. His sword wobbles in outstretched arms. From there, I grab his arm, breaking his guard, and plunge the dirk home.

The faint queasiness that always comes with a kill pushes forward, but like every other time, I can't acknowledge it because we're still in the thick of it. I pivot, finding Remy backed into the wall, sword pinned across his body and straining against Janvier. The elf leans into him, blade locked against Remy's, swirling power helping him leverage against the warlock.

The half-fae is down, probably hit by the blast Remy redirected.

For a moment, the magic tries its best to look like wildfire. But it passes, and I cover the distance in two strides, reaching through it and grabbing Janvier's shoulder, my knife striking at his throat.

Something punches my chest and I'm flung backward, skidding across the uneven alley pavement and shoulder impacting the brick wall. A sound wheezes from me and dampness soaks my shirt at my shoulder and chest.

Janvier stalks toward me, leaving Remy pinned against the wall by swirling magic. But my crewmate's face is twisted in concentration. It won't take him long to break through the holding spell and until then, I've got to fend off Janvier.

I struggle up, fingers numb around my knife. And immediately pitch to the side to avoid a bolt of crackling light. Shattered brick explodes and clips my side, stinging unprotected human skin again. I settle to a crouch, knife up and ready like that's going to counter the next magic attack.

Janvier prowls closer, elven magic twisted away from the normal *nurture* and *regeneration* slithering around his hands. It crackles and snaps, turned a sickly yellow-green. A direct hit from that might stop my heart.

"Andrew Minnare. Remember him?" he snarls.

I have absolutely no idea who he's talking about, and my honest "No," really infuriates him. I swivel away from the blast, part of it still clipping my arm. Weakness spiderwebs up the limb.

"You killed him two months ago, *shilsa*." Janvier leaps forward, calling up more magic. I lunge to meet him, dropping my shoulder and ramming it into his chest. Even without stoneskin, I make a good battering ram. Janvier is thrown backward, his spell flying free and rebounding around the narrow alley.

I duck, boot skidding on bloody rubble and sending me to a knee, my shoulder screaming as it again takes the brunt of my weight against a wall. Remy shouts and the comforting blue of his magic swarms the spell and suppresses it. He breaks the last bit of Janvier's spell pinning him and goes after the elf, their swords sparking silty green and blue with each clash. Janvier throws out a hand and the ground ripples under Remy's feet, throwing him to one knee.

Remy gets his hand up, and the heat of a catching spell hits me from three paces away. Janvier strains, trying to pull his sword free where it's locked midair. He's frozen long enough for me to lurch over and slam into him.

Remy has impeccable timing with the release as always and Janvier impacts the wall with a dull thud. He must have a whole host of protective wards around him, because he bounces back, leaving an elf-shaped impression in the brick.

He swings at me and his blade slices through the front of my jacket. I deflect the next thrust with my dirk. Janvier might still be standing after being tackled into a wall, but he's at least shaky on his feet. His next attack lacks any real threat, and I get under his guard and plunge the dirk at his chest.

My shoulder wrenches as something *stops* me. Janvier's wide eyes focus on the bloody dirk a bare inch from his chest, a sheen of red pushing back against me. I grit my teeth and push harder, trusting Remy to take care of whatever this new thing is.

It wobbles closer, but Janvier's free hand punches my chest and I'm shoved back a step.

I recover quicker and charge right back. He throws up an arm, right into my next attack. He screams as the blade pierces his forearm, posture collapsing and knife-pinned arm slamming against his chest as my momentum carries on. But again, it doesn't pierce his chest, protected by wards.

Claws sink into my shoulders and toss me to the ground. For the second time in the space of minutes, I'm gasping for breath. Remy's down behind me, but he scrambles to hands and knees, grabbing his basalt sword again, face bleeding and clothes smoking. I numbly follow his focused glare to the alley entrance where a woman stands.

Fire wicks around her feet, casting a scent like burning sewage. Janvier lurches toward her, and I realize too late that she's casting a gate circle, something that'll instantly transport them away. I try to get up, but my shoulder vengefully protests.

Janvier meets my gaze, and I've never seen such fury in someone's face. My dirk is still lodged in his arm. I go for the other knife on the belt across my chest, but they're already shimmering.

Remy shouts, trying to cast something. Janvier raises his hand, the same wild-eyed rage shining in his eyes. Wildfire erupts, shooting toward me.

Panic takes over, the flames all I can see. I twist, trying to curl away from it like that will protect me from its destructive path. Something solid slams into my chest, and Remy's arm smashes against my shoulder as he reaches over me.

Roaring fills my ears as wildfire hits his shield and breaks around it, grasping at open air before it fizzles out.

Then it's just harsh breaths with an edge of fear breaking from me, awkwardly sprawled on the ground. Remy grabs me and I reflexively clutch his arm.

"I got you, Bes."

My head thuds against his shoulder, leaning into the half-hug he's got me in for another second before trying to sit up. Remy helps me get upright. We're alone in the alley except for the bodies of the henchmen. Janvier and the other magic-user are long gone, a scorched circle on the ground the only mark left.

I cradle my arm against my chest and tip my chin at the mark. "Can you get anything off that?"

"Only after you tell me you're okay." He groans as he sits and extends his leg. He dabs at the bleeding cut on his cheek, winces, and then scrubs his jacket sleeve across sweaty forehead. He looks beat, and I *feel* it.

"Yeah. I'm—"

"Bleeding." He reaches over and tugs at my jacket. "Damn, Bes, what'd you get hit with?"

My shoulder has been the loudest, so I hadn't noticed the impact site at my chest and the bloody mess it's turning my shirt into. A wave of lightheadedness swoops over me and he grips my upper arm to keep me from keeling over.

"Hang tight, I'm calling Dejan."

"Okay," I sort of stupidly reply.

He shifts to balance on the balls of his feet, keeping one hand on my arm to support me, while he fishes out his phone.

"Ah, hell," he growls and shoves it away. A faint smile creeps over my face, and I manage to get mine out of my pocket and hand it over.

"Fried?" I ask.

He knows my passcode and keys it in, shaking his head. "Two weeks. I hate tech."

"I don't think they intend for them to be near alley fights or terrorist attacks."

He rolls his eyes, and lifts the phone to his ear, moving my jacket and checking other injuries. A frown creases between his eyes as he uncovers more that I'm also just noticing as the adrenaline fades.

Curling up on the ground and just passing out is sounding *really* good right about now. Except I need to pass on the name and Janvier's seething *"you killed him two months ago."*

"Dej, it's me," Remy says. "Bes is bleeding in about five places."

I can hear Dejan's "*What?*"

I'm not usually the one impaled in multiple places.

"Yeah, I'm good," Remy reassures as he stands with a grimace, and limps his way to the alley entrance. I start to push myself over to the wall to borrow its support. It's getting chillier. Though it could also be the delayed processing reaction to realizing that it's definitely not coincidence, and Janvier was probably tracking Cieran to get to me.

"Alley off Meadows between Eighth and Tenth." Remy makes his way back over. "We've got bodies. Janvier's in the wind. Again. There's a gate mark, so don't mess it up when you come in."

He slowly lowers to a knee beside me. "Okay, Dejan and Sarge are on their way. Let's get this off."

He reaches for my jacket, and I lean forward to help shrug it off. I curse for once as he works it around the forearm wound.

"You kiss your mom with that mouth?" Remy asks lightly. My lips flatten in mock annoyance. And to keep in another rare curse as we get the coat off.

"How'd this happen?" Remy folds it over his knee before gently helping shift my arm back to my chest.

I can't answer, can't tell him that for some reason my stoneskin's not kicking in when it needs to.

"Talk to me," he says and it's what I always say when they're off, and this time it doesn't infuriate me. Maybe I just needed to get beat up in an alley to admit to this. But before I can, Dejan slides around the corner, halfway jumping over the gate mark.

He's at my side, a paramedic bag thumping to the ground next to him. Cieran's there too, wide-eyed panic on his face before he registers me still awake and alert.

Before I can say anything, Dejan touches my chest, and something explodes through me. As darkness swallows me, I think I hear Nadire calling my name again.

12

NADIRE

I DON'T KNOW WHAT's more shocking. The destruction around me or my brother vanishing midair with barely a look back. I jolt forward like I can go grab him, bring him back.

"Hey!" Motion arrests me and it's Dejan, hands on my upper arms. I'm a few inches taller than him, but that's not hard since every Antilles is over six feet tall.

"What's..."

"He's okay," Dejan reassures, releasing me. "We're suddenly on duty." He gives a mirthless smile that makes me uneasy. On duty. Explosions and destroyed buildings. Terrorists apparently in my coffee shop.

"Was this because of me?" I ask. And it's only after it's out that I realize how stupid it sounds.

"Because he came into your café to tail us?" Dejan asks, voice gentler than I've ever heard from him. Usually he's barely stopping himself from cursing around us—and especially Mom—when he does talk.

"Well...yes." My shoulders slump and he bumps my arm with a closed fist before backing off.

"No, you are not personally responsible for a terrorist attack in a public space and your brother doing his job."

That gets a faint laugh from me. "That's really comforting when you put it that way."

Dejan flashes a wry smile. "I don't quite have Bes's gift with words."

I fold my arms across my chest, rubbing my hands against the comforting ridges of the knit sweater. Not many do.

He checks the street behind me. "You guys far enough down to avoid this?"

I nod, craning a look up at the damaged building above us. "We felt it for sure."

"Let's head over to the other side. I don't trust this." He jerks a thumb at the building. A few police officers are circling around, putting up crime-scene tape. Now that he mentions it, I feel like it's one slight breath away from collapsing on us.

We cross the street and join Cieran where he stiffly picks up a backpack. Besim's. Dust covers the sergeant, and he straightens with a grimace. It sends me further into shock to see them both so impacted when just minutes ago everything was normal and I was about to fight with my brother.

"Is Besim okay?" I ask quietly.

Dejan scoffs slightly. "That's a loaded question."

Cieran pulls the backpack on with a muffled groan. "Yeah, I noticed."

I want to shake them and tell them not to do the whole "talk in code" thing, because they've also noticed Besim's off and why aren't they doing anything about it?

But Dejan pulls his phone out of his back pocket. "Speaking of." He answers but his greeting dies and he's instantly alert.

"*What?*"

Cieran lurches like he wants to grab it and take over.

"Bes is hurt," Dejan says to him, ignoring the way the words pummel through me. "You good, Remy?"

My heart's in my chest and I'm about to grab the phone, demand to talk to my brother.

"Where are you?" Dejan beats us both to it. "Three blocks away, Meadows and Tenth," he tells Cieran. "On our way." He pockets the phone and looks around, crossing over to the nearest paramedic and scoops up the bag. "I need to borrow this, Mark."

And with that, he and Cieran take off running down the sidewalk, ignoring Mark's protests. A split second later, I'm following.

They leave me behind, but I heard the address and know which way to go. Dunhare's a grid, so it's a left turn down Meadows and three blocks straight down to Tenth. My days of a six-minute mile for high school volleyball are more than a few years behind me, so I'm panting by the time I see Cieran dodge into an alley. Five seconds later, I round the corner, coming up short.

Remy pivots on one knee, magic flaring around his outstretched hand. I freeze for the second it takes him to recognize me. Then he glances down at my feet and grimaces, hand clenching in a fist and extinguishing flames.

I'm in the middle of a charred ring and my sneakers have disrupted the neat coils. I hop out but I can tell by his face that it's much too late.

"I'm sorry!"

If he says something it's lost in the chaos of Dejan touching Besim's chest, him jerking like he got hit by a lightning strike, and going limp as I scream his name.

Cieran grabs me and holds me back as Dejan pulls a knife and cuts Besim's shirt open, not panicking as far as I can tell.

Remy keeps Besim propped up against the wall as Dejan works. And I stare helplessly at the ugly wounds across his chest, blood running from the arm limp beside him, and the burn scars painfully visible.

It's the same sort of helplessness as seeing him in the hospital for the first time, bandages everywhere, face pale, and not okay like he always is.

"What happened?" Cieran asks.

"Some sort of delayed shock spell. Missed it." Dejan hisses and shakes out his hand as something sparks. "Almost got it." He overlaps his hands and pushes them against the injury again, lips moving silently for much too long, before fingers curl and he pulls an invisible something off Besim and slams it into the ground.

Besim twitches, but doesn't wake up. Dejan grabs bandage packs and hands them to Remy. The warlock keeps a shoulder against Besim's as he starts to unwrap them.

"How'd that get through his stoneskin?" Dejan asks.

"I didn't ever see it during the fight," Remy answers, passing some gauze over.

"He should have mail on, too." Dejan shakes his head, light green elven magic covering his hand as he passes it over the gouges on Besim's chest.

"He doesn't really need it though, does he?" Remy replies.

"Apparently, he *firren* does." Dejan grabs more gauze and pushes it against the injury which already looks so much better.

"I don't know, Dej, he's not *firren talking*." Apparently easy-going Remy can get pissed off, and it's amazing that it's not the elf snapping at him but my brother instead who's causing it.

"Is he okay?" I whisper.

Dejan grabs a roll of surgical tape and rips a few pieces, securing the bandage, and moving on to the gaping wound on Besim's forearm.

"Told him that *firren* move would get him," Dejan mutters. Remy shakes his head, holding Besim's arm per Dejan's instructions as the elf gets to work again.

Cieran still watches in silence, but it seems like he's a million miles away.

"Is he okay?" I ask louder, and no one answers. I'm about to yell when Cieran stirs.

"Dej?"

The elf dumps bloody gauze on the ground, Besim's forearm marginally cleaner than before.

"He will be. Should wake up soon. You want to chew him out, *Sergeant*, or should I?" Dejan throws a challenging look over his shoulder at Cieran, and I want to distance myself from it.

But Cieran doesn't react. "He need a hospital?"

Dejan shifts his grip on Bes's arm, closing his eyes. Magic flares around his hands for seconds before Dejan opens his eyes again, shaking his head slightly like he's clearing it. Remy frowns at him and hands over more gauze. But the edges of the ragged wound are much neater, partially closed up.

"He'll be okay with somewhere to lie down for a bit. I'll monitor him." Dejan's voice is calmer, or maybe it's the amount of magic he just expended to heal my brother.

"My place isn't far," Cieran says. "But it might be watched."

"Janvier left with Bes's dirk through his arm. He might have other concerns right now." Remy shifts Besim forward for Dejan to check his shoulder.

And with that horrifying bit of information, I actually look around the alley. There's scorch marks everywhere, darker spatters that mirror the stains around Besim, and *oh saints...bodies.*

I jolt away, and hands guide me farther into the alley, helping steady me as I heave but nothing comes up. For once my habit of skipping breakfast when I'm rushed works in my favor.

"I'll get my car," Remy says behind me and boots retreat.

Cieran taps my shoulder. "You good?"

I scrub my sleeve over my mouth, trying to wipe out the taste of threatening bile. "Yeah," I tell him.

"Okay, hang out right here." Cieran's presence disappears and it takes a second to nerve myself up to turn around and focus *just* on Besim and nothing else.

My phone buzzing in my pocket has my heart jolting back up into my throat, but I grab it and answer to Maya's panicked, "Where are you?"

"I'm okay! I'm sorry!" I push my hand against my forehead, trying to break through the swarming lightheadedness. "Something happened with Besim and I'm with him right now."

"He okay?"

I look at him and my hand clutches around the St. Benedict medal hanging on the chain under my sweater. As I do, he stirs slightly, and his eyes crack open.

"Yeah." My voice shakes still. "The guys are with him."

"Nadi?"

"Um." I sniff. "Just close up and go home. It's going to be too crazy around there for anyone to be by."

"You sure?"

"Yeah. I'll figure out pay coverage and stuff since shifts will be short." I'm already trying to, somehow, in this alley full of carnage. But it's better than focusing on the death.

"Nadi, seriously, don't. I'll just take the lower check this week. You don't need to."

But I do, for no other reason than it would feel like admitting I have a very tenuous hold on everything. "I'll check in later. Can you do everything yourself?"

"Yeah," she reassures. "Just make sure your brother is okay."

"Thanks."

I hang up, and find Besim's bleary gaze settled on me.

"What are you doing here?" He's all sorts of confused, eyes squinting and words slurring. But tears threaten at seeing him awake and somewhat coherent.

"I heard you got hurt, stupid, so I came to make sure you were okay."

His head rests against the wall and his eyes close again, blinking back open before I can panic.

"What's the diagnosis, Dej?" he asks, voice clearer.

"That you're *firren* stupid." Dejan starts to pack bloody gauze and unused bandage tape into the bag.

Besim rolls his eyes, then immediately stiffens. "Where's Remy?"

Cieran crouches next to him, jacket in hand. "Went to go get a car. We're regrouping, and I guess finding you a new shirt."

Besim frowns at Dejan who just spreads his hands. "Wear mail next time, *shilsa*."

Besim opens his mouth but Cieran and Dejan as one tug up their jacket sleeves to show the cuff of a chain mail shirt. Nausea stirs again.

They'd been wearing those when they were in the *Fox*, maybe even expecting some sort of attack.

Besim's mouth tugs the way it does when he knows he's outmaneuvered. "I've got a shirt in my backpack."

Cieran obligingly takes it off and starts rummaging through pockets.

"You're such a boy scout," I say, and Besim flashes a tired smile back. Cieran pulls out a dark grey shirt as an old green Explorer rumbles to a stop and Remy gets out. Dejan takes over helping Besim as soldiers follow Remy into the alley.

The two newcomers are in dark grey fatigues, and chain mail glints under armored tac vests bearing the Drax Guard seal.

"Sergeant," one drawls, and Cieran's mouth flattens. Dejan and Besim exchange some *look* that has a laugh bubbling up. I'm really sure I'm not supposed to let it out.

Instead I shoulder Bes's backpack and offer an arm to help him start getting up. He slowly does and leans more on Dejan than me. We start to move around Cieran where he's talking to this new soldier whose tone is the textbook definition of condescending. Remy squats on the edge of the circle, frowning and brushing fingers over the lines.

The other soldier hovers above him and Remy flicks a glance up, sending the same *look* to his teammates and I really do almost laugh this time. But the sight of my footprint marring the circle sobers me.

"Did I ruin it?" I ask sheepishly. Whatever *it* was and whatever he needed it for.

Remy offers a tight smile. "It'll be okay."

"Letting civvies ruin evidence?" The soldier clicks his tongue and Remy smoothly rises to his feet, eyes narrowing slightly at the man. I tug at Besim, trying to get him moving faster because I really don't want to be here to see anything happen that would ruin the impression I have of all three of them being...you know...harmless, super muscular guys who'll just offer to punch a boyfriend or something.

"Jacobs." Besim nods as we move by. "Looking spotless as always."

Remy's mouth twitches and a definite snicker comes from Dejan. I bite down on my tongue to prevent a cackle of laughter.

The warlock opens the car door and Besim carefully levers in, Dejan following. Cieran circles around, pausing once on the other side of the hood.

"Get in." He nods at me.

I don't need a second invitation, not really wanting to walk back alone. And definitely not wanting to be left with the scowling soldiers.

I cram in, murmuring an apology to Dejan for being stuck between Besim and me in the backseat. He mutters something and then some-how—probably being a much smaller elf—manages to move himself into the cargo space without kicking us.

"Oh good, the booster seat's back there, Dej." Remy throws the car in gear and pulls out.

Dejan braces himself against the seat and flips Remy off in the rearview. The warlock's smirk is mirrored on the others' faces. I reach over and touch Besim's arm, hopefully not messing up the bandages or anything.

"I'm good," he promises. But it doesn't really seem that way as he tips his head back against the headrest. Dejan wordlessly reaches forward again, pressing Besim's shoulder. Besim taps his hand with a fist and the elf withdraws.

It's so simple, this relationship he has with all of them. Mostly word-less, because he gives Remy a small nod as the warlock checks over his shoulder. It's similar to the way we all check on each other. But not the same at all, because we've never taken a beaten-up sibling out of an alley where he was fighting, and apparently stabbing, literal terrorists and not bothered by it at all. It makes me compress into my seat.

How much do any of us really know Besim at all?

13

NADIRE

I DON'T REALLY PAY attention as Remy drives. The others are quiet. Besim closes his eyes, and it seems like he fell asleep in two seconds except his breath is too regulated to be relaxed. Cieran leans an elbow against the car window, rubbing his chin, only talking to give Remy directions.

And I'm left holding Besim's backpack in my lap, his computer taking up blocky space inside. Communications Specialist. That's what his title is. We all know that. And somehow I guess I thought that meant he was outside the fighting. And maybe it made me mad when I saw him in the hospital and had to actually confront the fact that he goes into the thick of it.

We pull to a stop and I blink, staring at the neighborhood around us. I'd figured we'd be going to the Army base instead. Cieran is out first, looking up and down the quiet street, before heading up a short walk to unlock the door of a brick house with blue trim around the windows.

Remy cracks his door as soon as Cieran nods and that seems to be the signal for me to also move. I don't want to mess anything else up, even if it's just getting out of a car. Cieran gets Besim's door and helps him stand. I circle around, hovering anxiously and still clutching the backpack to my chest.

Remy opens the back hatch and Dejan slides out, bringing the paramedic bag with him.

"Whose bag did you steal?" Remy asks.

Dejan slings it over his shoulder. "Mark's."

"Who's Mark?"

"Someone who's going to want his bag back eventually."

Besim shakes his head as he leans on Cieran and they make for the door. "Sure this is okay, Sarge?" he asks.

"We're already here, Bes," Cieran replies. "Go sit." He points to the couch as soon as we're in the small entryway. It opens to a living area on our right and a cozy dining room on our left. Besim obeys and the other two come in, still talking about the bag and sounding so much like our younger brothers.

Maybe this is why it's hard for me to see them as super elite soldiers when they're bickering about someone's bag that Dejan technically stole.

Cieran locks the door and Remy turns and presses his hand against the wood. A few runes glow and then fade into the wood. He nods to Cieran and keeps arguing with Dejan without missing a beat.

I'm still standing, not sure what I'm doing here.

Besim sits down and Cieran reappears with a pillow and thick quilt and tosses them to him.

"Lie down."

He passes around the couch as Besim punches the pillow once and obeys, wincing as he does. The sergeant reappears from another doorway and tosses a small bottle at Dejan who catches it and measures out two small pills to give to Besim and then pops one himself.

"Want any?" he asks Remy. The warlock shakes his head, and the motion makes me actually look him in the eye.

"Your face is bleeding," I say.

"Was. It's okay," he reassures.

"Want me to take care of it right now?" Dejan catches the blanket Cieran tosses him. He looks at it in confusion.

"No, just sometime before I go home and Bear sees me," the warlock replies. "I think that means you need to lie down since you overdid it with the magic." He points to the blanket.

"Sure does." Cieran takes the backpack from me. Dejan scowls at both of them but takes himself to the smaller couch and curls up on it, drawing the blanket over his head.

"What do you need?" the sergeant asks and it takes a second to register he's asking me.

"Um...I..." My hands are moving and I'm just now noticing I'm still in my café apron, pocket holding some peppermint candy I was going to use to garnish the tops of mochas.

"Bathroom is through there." He points me past the couches to another short hallway. My feet are carrying me before I fully agree to the course, and I shut the door behind me. Wide eyes look back from the mirror and my hair is still in the terrible bun. I don't know why *I'm* the one two seconds from a panic attack when I just stood there for all of it.

It takes a few minutes and water splashed across my face before some steadiness comes back. I make my way back to the foyer, following the scent of fresh coffee. Besim and Dejan are both asleep, and I pause. Besim's on his side, face turned into the pillow, injured arm carefully tucked up next to his chest. The burn scars on his neck, staking a faint claim along his jaw, and tucking under his shirt collar are fully visible.

I know the basics of magic and identifying types that we all learn in grade school, but whatever got him, it had to have gone *through* his stoneskin...the thing Remy said hadn't appeared while they were fighting. The thing I *know* Besim always uses after seeing him get into scrapes growing up. It's automatic, a protective reaction. I didn't know it could actually be suppressed.

No wonder he's not doing okay.

Why isn't he talking to anyone about it? Why not us? I cross my arms in a burst of anger. It fades just as fast. That's rich coming from me, the person who doesn't talk to anyone, trying to do it all herself.

I turn away, stepping down a shallow ledge into the dining room. It's separated from the kitchen by a tall bar. Remy sits in one of the tall chairs tucked under the edge on the dining side, leaning forward on the granite surface, head pillowed on his arms. Cieran's in the kitchen itself, another small step up.

"Water?" I ask.

He turns to a cabinet and pulls out a glass, pointing to the sink. I fill it and back out of his way as he grabs a mug and pours hot water. He sets it beside Remy who lifts his head and looks confused at the hot tea brewing next to him.

"Unless you want coffee?" Cieran tosses a bag of chocolate chips beside it. Remy shakes his head and returns to the same positioning.

Cieran leans back against the counter, waiting for the coffee to finish brewing. Bright pictures on the fridge catch my eye, and I'm looking before I can help myself.

Cieran stands with three other men, in full gear, and grinning out. He's got the same hat on but looks...happy. I swallow hard as I realize he's with Crew Six right now and these guys in the picture are nowhere to be seen. Besim had said something about Cieran being assigned for the last mission since he didn't have a crew...

I turn away from the picture, eye catching him and one of the same guys in dress blues. Skim away to him and a woman laughing in a picture. Her, I do know.

"You used to come in with her." I point to it, twisting to bring him into view.

"Yeah." He half-smiles. "That's my sister."

It's the quiet way he says it, the way he crosses his arms tight over his chest, the way Remy lifts his head slightly again to check on him. My heart squeezes as it dips down toward my toes.

"I'm really sorry," I whisper. I can't seem to do much right today. Or any day.

Cieran smiles again, sadness still mixed inside it. "Thanks." He shifts his arms, and his boot scuffs the ground. "She really liked your place. She was obsessed with those cake things...some sort of sesame something." He shakes his head.

I brighten. "The black sesame cardamom buns?"

"Those."

Remy lifts his head higher. "That sounds amazing."

"They really are," I tell him. "Our sister makes them." I twist like I can encompass Besim with the action.

"You should bring them back. They're really good," Cieran says.

"Oh. Yeah." I rub my upper arms again. They hadn't been in the little glass pastry case in a while. "I won't bore you with sibling politics."

He tilts his head, and it feels like he sees right through the excuse, much like Besim can.

"Can I bum some coffee off you?" I try for cheery. He brings out two more pottery mugs, matching the one Remy bobs the tea bag in—white glazed with bluebonnets painted around the outside.

And it brings a smile from me, these guys drinking from mugs so different than them.

"Sorry, I'm not fancy, so it's black coffee. Milk in the fridge if you want."

I take the cup and find the milk, adding a splash. Remy extends his hand and I offer the carton. He dumps some in his tea and hands it back.

"Thanks."

The warlock checks the bag label before dumping out some chocolate chips onto the counter. He plucks two and pops them in his mouth with an expression of vague suffering. Weirdo.

I blow on my coffee before trying a sip. And I can't help it. "These are really pretty mugs."

Cieran smirks over the rim of his. "Thanks." He sets the mug on the counter and crosses his arms again. "I got them for Shay, if you can believe it."

"Good eye." I salute him by lifting the mug. He tips his head to acknowledge.

"Everything else in here was her." He casts a wistful look around the kitchen. This must have been her house, and from the look on his face he can't quite decide if it's better or worse to live with the ghosts of her all around.

"It's really nice." It's the sort of place that feels lived in—books on the shelves, blankets in every room, pictures on the refrigerator, a box of fruit loops on the counter.

"Is that you and a tiger?" Remy studies the hand-drawn pictures on colorful construction paper, brow creased. It looks similar to the one his son drew Besim a while ago.

Cieran chuckles. "Yeah, Javi's kids made them for me a few weeks ago when I was in the hospital."

Remy huffs. "That's awesome."

"And Masood's wife brought over a five-course meal she just 'happened to have lying around,' so if you're hungry at all, please help me eat it."

Remy laughs softly and snugs the mug between his hands, shoulders hunching up to his ears as he leans on the counter. He's finished off the chocolate, but doesn't look in a hurry to get more. I look back at the photo of Cieran and the other soldiers and swallow a lump in my throat.

"You been around?" Remy asks.

"A few times," Cieran replies. "It's still just...hard."

"Yeah." An acknowledgment comes from Remy, and I still can't look away from the picture and the ghosts, wondering if that will one day be Besim or if he'll be one of the missing. What would happen if he was the one left behind? Or if Remy or Dejan were?

"You know, it was good having a sergeant out there," Remy says carefully. I'm in the middle of something, probably in the way, but they're not moving the conversation or excluding me.

A sigh cuts from Cieran. "Still thinking on it."

I manage to pull my focus from the crew picture, sipping coffee to cover the watering in my eyes.

"Are you going to be the new sergeant?" I ask. Besim hadn't been too happy when his old sergeant had retired months ago.

Cieran lifts his shoulders.

"I think...I just..." I'm holding a mug in his kitchen, trying to say something and I'm not even sure what it is. All I know is I haven't been great at things, have been kind of an asshole to my brother, and I'm looking at a few people who might know him better than any of us.

"Is Besim okay?" I finally ask.

Cieran inclines his head to Remy, deflecting the question.

The warlock gives a tight smile. "No. But he's not talking to us, so I assume he's not talking to you guys."

I shake my head, the implication stinging—that Besim would go to them first. But Remy didn't bat an eye about the alley fight or the blood still crusting his cheek.

"This is going to sound *so* trite and stupid." Another glance at the photo and then back to some point between where the two of them lean on the counter. "You know it's just...you don't really think about what he does, what you guys do. And he always comes back." A breath shudders from me. "Then one day you get a call...Besim's in the hospital, and you go, and he's...he's really hurt. The brother you think is invincible since he's always been there, you know?"

My hands clench around the mug. "And then he's not himself, he's just *off*, and I don't know what to do about it."

"If it makes you feel better, it's kind of the same for us." Remy offers a faint smile. And something in me is relieved that he's actually talking to me, and we can exist in the same space without me being a mess because I'm trying to get him to notice me.

"I guess he sort of needs someone to look out for him." I look to Cieran. "Because obviously we're not doing a very good job." The words pull a sniff from me.

"Hey," Cieran says gently. "We all keep it separate. What we do and family. It's lines we don't want to get crossed."

Remy nods, and my cheeks heat, the way I've never really thought about it.

"But um..." Cieran clears his throat. "The last crew I looked out for ended up dead, so..." There's a flash of brightness in his eyes as he dips his focus to the floor and then back to me after a second to regain control. "It'll just take time."

It seems directed more at Remy than me.

For a minute, I wish I was more like Besim. Able to give the right words of comfort or reassurance. The fact that I'm not, and realizing I've been wanting to hear him say *I'm* doing okay, makes me miss him even more. Like he's gone and not asleep in the next room. But it feels like he's been miles away. I wonder how long he's felt like that.

My phone buzzes again, and I pull it out with an apologetic look. *Mom.*

"Hey, Mom." My voice wavers.

"Nadi! I'm so glad you picked up! The neighbor came over and told me there'd been some attack downtown and Taron said they'd heard it was by your café. Are you okay?" She finishes breathless and poised to ask again when I take an extra second to swallow the same tightness.

"Yeah, I'm okay. It was a few blocks down the street." I'm not looking at the guys and the way they seem to lean toward me.

"Oh, thank the Lord," Mom whispers and I know she's lighting candles at the small Sacred Heart nook we've had in the house all my life. "Are you still down there? Do you want someone to come get you? Do you want to come over here?"

It makes my eyes sting again. I really do need to stop being so stubborn and go home more often.

"I got a ride from Besim and his crew, and closed down everything for today."

There's a breathless pause that makes me wince, and then, "Was Besim down there too?"

"Yes." I can't really bring myself to say more, because I'm not telling her that he's in the other room, bandaged up again. I don't want to send her back into the worried frenzy that had her at the hospital as often as she could between offering novenas and going to Mass, praying her mother's heart out for her boy. "He's okay."

"Is he able to talk?" she asks carefully.

I don't know how to answer, so I look to the guys. "Is Besim able to talk?" Trying to keep my voice even, like everything is normal and he's standing right there.

Remy defers to Cieran, who shifts his arms tight again. I wonder if he's had to have this conversation with other worried families before. "We were first on the scene. Besim's working, but he'll call as soon as he has a chance."

I relay it and I feel like Mom doesn't really believe me based on the way her "Okay," echoes across the line. "Why don't you come over, Nadi? I'll make lunch."

Lunch. It feels like it should be midnight, but it's barely nine in the morning. And I really want to see her. See Dad when he comes home because it's Thursday and he always comes home for Thursday lunch, no matter what's going on at the construction site he's running.

"I'll be over in a bit. I'll see if one of them can give me a ride."

Remy nods and it feels settled.

"Okay. Love you, kiddo."

"Love you too, Mom. I'll tell Bes to call you."

One more "I love you," and she hangs up.

I hedge between my feet as I slide the phone away. "Um...can I hang out for a bit until he wakes up?"

"Yeah," Cieran replies. "Make yourself at home."

I manage a smile of thanks and make my way back out to the living room. I've nearly cried in front of them five times in as many minutes, so I'd rather take my chances with the sleeping soldiers in the other room.

A cushioned window seat provides blankets and a little shelf for a mug. I slide my sneakers off and curl into the seat, grabbing a quilt and folding it across my knees.

My head rests back, and my hands cup around my mug. I focus on the dormant flower beds outside that look like they've been well kept. It makes me sad for a woman I only met in passing. One who liked my café and black sesame buns and laughing with her brother, probably never thinking she was going to leave him behind.

I close my eyes and whisper a prayer for departed souls, hoping someone up there is looking out for a lonely-looking soldier surrounded by ghosts.

The coffee is gone, and my eyes are slowly blinking closed against the backdrop of muted and sporadic conversation from the kitchen when Dejan startles awake.

He and the blanket fight for a second before he sits up, rubbing bleary eyes and scrubbing a hand through blond hair, leaving it disheveled. He notices me and lips flatten as his head tips—the groggiest "hi" I ever seen.

Dejan stumbles over to Besim, still asleep, and tugs the blanket back. I swing my feet off the window seat, watching carefully. Darker green shimmers around Dejan's fingers and he lightly presses them to Besim's forehead. Apparently satisfied, he rests his hand on Besim's shoulder. The sharp scent of magic, something like the tang mint leaves behind, fills the room. Besim twitches but doesn't wake.

The elf flips the blanket back and moves around the couch.

"Thanks." My low murmur stops him. He regards me a moment, then dips his head and heads for the kitchen.

"Coffee?" his groggy voice asks and voices answer. I rest forearms against my legs, still waiting on Besim.

It's another few minutes before his voice rumbles out, "Your face is going to get stuck like that."

My head whips up from where I'd been frowning at the empty coffee mug clenched between my hands.

"You okay?" I rise to my feet, a half step away as he starts to get upright.

"I think so." He rocks his shoulder in a small circle. "Though falling asleep might have made it better *and* worse."

I set the mug on the low table and sit next to him. "Dejan did something for you a few minutes ago."

Besim glances at the empty couch, and then briefly over his shoulder. "He did?"

"I don't know, magic stuff, I guess."

He chuckles and it eases the lines around his face.

"I was really worried for a bit," I confess. His arm encircles my shoulders and tugs me close.

"I'm okay, promise. All in one piece."

I tip my head against him. "I know. But…it's just…I don't think you're really okay."

He pulls away and I'm about to curse my mouth again, when he sighs. "Yeah." He slumps forward and I've also never seen him look *defeated*.

"You know everyone's here for you, right?" This time I reach out, gingerly wrapping my arm around him, not really knowing what's going to hurt or not.

"I know." His shoulder nudges me. "Guess I'm not used to really leaning on anyone."

And he pins me with a bona fide Besim look.

"Okay," I mutter. "Point taken."

He chuckles and, a second later, my low laugh joins his.

"Sorry I've been kind of an asshole recently," I say.

He straightens and starts to stand. I rise with him, hand out in case he needs help.

"Apology accepted. And I've been out of it, too." He opens his arms, and I step in for a full hug. "You doing okay?" he asks.

"Yeah." I snug my arms tighter for a second before releasing. "Remy said he'd give me a ride to Mom and Dad's. She called when she heard the news, and told me to come over."

He arches an eyebrow and I'm not sure which part that's for.

"Don't worry." I sneak a glance across the foyer, making sure they're all out of earshot. "I'm probably swearing off anything to do with military guys."

Besim's smile creases again, and I push on. "We told Mom you were busy and would call later."

"Okay, thanks."

He huffs when I slam into him again for another hug. "Please be careful with whatever you guys are doing next."

I'm halfway hoping he's going to tell me that they're off the case, won't be going silent with phones off and no mention of when they might be back until we get a text or a call letting us know he's headed home. But he doesn't.

"We will."

He slowly leads the way to the kitchen, and his crew's faces all clear when they see him. Even Cieran smiles in relief.

"You ready to go?" Remy asks me. The message is clear. They've got things to do, and they can't have me around for it. I don't want to be around for it.

"Head back to base after," Cieran tells him. "We'll meet you there."

Remy nods and grabs his keys. I get one gentle punch to Besim's arm and give thanks to the others, and then we're out the door, headed somewhere safe and away from whatever dangerous thing they're going to run straight at without blinking.

14

Besim

"WELL?" CIERAN ASKS ME.

I huff and ease down onto one of the bar chairs, bracing my arms against the counter. He's cleaned up, new hoodie on and hat mostly free of dust. Dejan nurses a cup of coffee and sits on the counter. An opened bag of chocolate chips slouches next to him. He must be tired or decided he's going to trust Cieran completely to start perching.

"Well," I say. "Dejan looks like crap, so how much did you expend on me?"

Dejan tilts his head up, revealing circles under his eyes that weren't there this morning, but his jaw sets in its normal stubborn tilt.

"Enough for you to not need a hospital," he replies.

My mouth purses and he sends a challenging look back.

"I've never had to do that for you, so..." He leaves it hanging out in the open. If it were Remy, they'd already be bickering about it, but it's me, and usually *I'm* the one pushing to make sure he's not closing himself off.

"Guess they got lucky." The moment in the alley of wanting to confess is gone. Maybe it's still the dull ache clinging to my bones or the way they're looking at me, worried I might break, but it's making me clam up.

And even though I know things like this don't go well when kept inside, it seems like this might be the one time it's okay to keep hidden.

Cieran hums and it makes me want to hunch my shoulders.

"You know," he starts. "A few weeks ago, someone told me that no one's ever really alone, and made me talk about some things that made it better."

I focus on the marbled pattern of the granite for a moment, a mirror of what my skin should look like. Except there's a faultline running through me. "Well." I look up. "He sounds like an idiot."

"He might be for not taking his own advice." Cieran pins me with a look that makes me want to squirm. It's a commanding officer look, but I don't think he'll actually order me to talk.

"Where's your stoneskin, Bes?" Dejan cuts through the brief silence that's my ongoing refusal to say anything. Cieran flicks a look to him, then focuses back on me. Not brushing the question away and not letting me out of it either.

Pothos was somewhat gentler about these things. Or maybe he was just the type to ignore it too, and that's why it was more my job to keep eyes on everyone else. Though why I'd ever decided it was *my* job in the first place...

"It's fine," I say.

Dejan's jaw works for a moment, something flashing in his eyes, before he grits out an "Is it?"

I don't break off the glare he's giving me. Not until Cieran's quiet, "Dejan," draws the elf's attention.

"Sergeant," he spits back. Cieran slants his head slightly in a "stand down" motion, and it feels like Dejan might start sniping at Cieran instead. But he shrugs and tosses back another drink of coffee.

I scrub my hand across my forehead. Now that I'm up and avoiding things again, there's a faint headache trying to invade, held at bay by the healing magic Dejan used on me minutes ago according to Nadire. Memory is a little blurry and I don't actually remember much of the ride over here.

But one thing is coming back. *Andrew Minnare. You killed him two months ago.*

"You know the name 'Andrew Minnare'?" I ask Cieran.

The sergeant thinks a moment, turning to place his empty mug in the sink before he shakes his head. "Why?"

I rub my forehead again. The headache is really trying to invade. Dejan thumps off the counter and reaches over to me. I forestall him with a lift of my hand. He looks awful and I don't want him pouring more magic into me before his is replenished. And I don't want to flinch in front of them the way I did on the street.

He frowns at me and flicks a glance at Cieran. I'm not really sure if it's to check if Cieran will override me, or if the sergeant will stop Dejan if he tries to get the jump on me again.

I keep one eye on Dejan but the elf backs off slightly. "Janvier said I killed him two months ago."

They both stiffen and Cieran pushes away from the counter. "The Wastelands?"

"Must be," I say. "I don't know who he's talking about. The name didn't come up on any lists yesterday. But I didn't check the after-reports from the mission." The ones filed by Remy and Dejan and supplemented by the dragonwalkers. As well as the reports from the cleanup team who went out and recovered bodies and swept Andrej's lair.

Cieran scrapes a hand across his jaw. "I don't like where this is going."

We don't say it, but coincidence never really exists in our line of work.

"Let's head back to base. We'll need a more comprehensive report for Wolfe and to start setting our next moves. Dejan says you should be good to go."

It's not a question, it's a challenge, and one I dodge away from again. "Let's go."

————

Our CO is, understandably, miffed that we didn't come back to the tower immediately after the attack, even though Cieran had called him when we arrived at the house and when we left. But Cieran isn't backing down, defending his decision and making sure it rests squarely on him. Dejan and I shift slightly where we stand, a pace behind our fill-in-sergeant while Wolfe gives him a lecture.

"No more tiptoeing around. I have clearance for open and direct intervention as needed." Wolfe finally turns back to the mission.

Which means lethal force as needed and not worrying about making news.

"Yes, sir." Cieran nods, and I wonder if it weighs on him, accepting orders like those and giving them eventually.

Wolfe flicks a glance at us, frowning slightly like he did when he heard Remy is delivering my sister home.

"And I need you to decide, Sergeant."

It's unyielding, and Cieran's posture suddenly tries to lean away from it and the way Wolfe presses steepled fingers against the desk.

"Sir?" The same mulish avoidance I've been feeling soaks Cieran's voice.

"If you're taking the posting permanently or not. You're with Crew Six until this gets taken care of, and then I want an answer."

"Yes, sir."

I can't see his face, but I don't need to the way his shoulders line up, squaring off with something he's going to keep putting off until it hits him square in the face.

Once we're out of here, old me would be asking if he's okay, if he wants to talk through anything. But present me is a raging mess and avoiding my own issues with the skill of a ninja.

"Dismissed. I want a report as soon as you have something."

"Sir." We salute and make our way out into the hallway. Dejan, remarkably, doesn't say anything. Maybe waiting for me to initiate, but Cieran strides down the hall, hand with dampener bracelet clenching like mad. Finally he turns.

"Find a briefing room and start running that name. I'll be back in five minutes."

And he's gone, ducking through a stairwell door.

"Think he's going to take the discharge?" Dejan asks, staring after him. I'm not sure what's going through the elf's head. Sometimes it's really hard to parse out. But he's talking to me and it's without the accusation of earlier, so I lean into feeling useful.

"You want him to stick around?" I return and get a raised eyebrow and brief purse of lips. It's one beat off from the "therapy voice" he complains about.

But he answers. "I don't know." He lapses into silence, but I wait, and eventually he talks again. "You know, crew team-ups in the past always went well."

I shake my head slightly. If "well" meant we all made it home, then yes.

"The Wastelands mission was a shitty thing to send him into, even when it was just a patrol." Dejan crosses his arms tight, still looking at the door. "But I'd rather someone grieving than pretending he's fine and that losing people didn't gut him."

Cieran doesn't BS, and that's why Dejan likes him.

"And?"

Dejan lifts a shoulder. "And Remy wants him as sergeant, so...probably should trust that."

I offer a slight smile. Even through Hell Week, the thing that forged men into brothers before missions cemented it, Remy and Dejan didn't get along. At all.

Until the first mission, when we were just a newly formed crew. Dejan didn't trust Remy's judgment and only Remy's reflexes and magic shield saved the both of them. And after they'd picked themselves off the ground, Remy had punched Dejan in the face. The elf shrugged, and slapped a healing spell on the warlock's bleeding knuckles and dislocated shoulder.

They've been close ever since.

"And?"

He huffs, sending me a flat glare that holds no ice.

"And I don't want a promotion." A promotion that would end his job as team medic, something he holds fiercely despite seeming the sort of person who'd rather rely only on sword and bow and attack magic than gentler healing spells. "Or to get split up."

"Fair enough," I say.

"Same for you?" he asks.

I nod slowly. Cieran O'Donnell ran a crew you were always ready to be paired with for missions, sometimes the riskiest ones, because you knew he'd be making sure everyone got out if he could. His team followed without blinking, sometimes laughing as they went. He remembered every detail, covered every angle, and cared. Pranks, jokes, mundane things, life, missions, family. He cared.

"Yeah. Same for me."

The elevator door at the end of the hall slides open and Remy steps out, brown paper bag in hand and from the smell, laden with naan and spiced meats and vegetables from the Pakistani elf food truck down the street.

"Where's Sarge?" he asks, joining us as I pick a briefing room from among the four branching off from the hall.

"Taking five," Dejan replies as we filter in.

Remy winces. "Briefing was that bad?"

Dejan's eyebrow arches as he slides a chair back with a foot. "And CO told him he needed to make a decision about staying or leaving."

The warlock shakes his head, starting to pull out smaller containers from the bag and setting them on the table. I get my computer out of the backpack Cieran salvaged from the street, and cautiously open it, scared of what I might find after landing on top of it.

The hinge creaks warningly, and it opens with a bit of a wobble. There's a hairline crack down the right edge of the screen, but it comes to life and doesn't seem to have been affected by whatever magic Remy was throwing around.

But I usually invest in getting magic dampeners for my tech, knowing who I spend most of my time with.

Speaking of. "Where's your phone, Rem?"

He slides the dead phone across the table, before continuing to portion out food into one of the smaller serving bowls. Dejan does the same in the seat next to me.

"Another one?" he asks.

Remy tears a piece of naan. "Shut up."

I put in the request for evidence from the detectives, and since I already have access to the cameras on the street from a prior request, I log in again and download the footage to see what we missed. Then key in a search for the name *Andrew Minnare.*

While waiting, I get out the small kit I keep around, take a screwdriver, and pry off the back of the phone. A bowl filled to the brim appears in my periphery and Dejan sticks a plastic fork, tines down, into it.

"Thanks," I tell him as I frown at the mess of circuit boards and power crystals inside the phone. One of the tiny crystals is in smaller pieces than it should be, and tiny scorch marks overlay circuit boards and some wiring. "Uh...you were thorough, Rem."

The warlock groans and mumbles a curse on technology through a full mouth.

"I'm also not seeing the dampener I gave you." I glance up.

"Hadn't got around to putting it in yet," he admits.

"Sounds like your fault then." Dejan stabs a chunk of beef, dipping into the spicier sauce.

Remy gives him a withering look, which Dejan ignores with a smirk.

"You have a spare?" I switch the phone for food and dig in.

"At home."

"You can use mine." Dejan puts his on the table.

"Thanks." Remy doesn't make a move for it yet, and I don't blame him. He and his son live with his parents, and they have to have seen the news by now, and are probably panicking that they can't reach him. But they have all our numbers too, and we haven't gotten a terrified call.

But from what Wolfe had said, and showed us screenshots of, we were definitely caught on camera by the news agencies. Maybe they figure he's working.

And Dejan? Dejan has us.

The laptop chimes, and I check to make sure it's nothing more than hits and requested updates coming through, before turning back to eating. Cieran needs to be in here before we do anything, and I'd rather focus on food and the guys right here before anything else.

It's another five minutes before Cieran steps through the open door.

"Smells good," he says, nudging the door shut.

"Help yourself." Remy starts to fill a bowl despite his words. Cieran slowly sits next to him, maybe cautious that we'll bring up the sergeant posting again, but we're all just focused on eating. Like it's been days since we've had anything.

And it's still more minutes later when Cieran finally slows long enough to ask, "What do we have?"

I glance at the laptop. Reports and notifications are coming in. But Remy beats me to it.

"The container got smashed in the fight, but I got a few face-fulls of Janvier's magic to know it was him who tagged the café," he says. "I pulled a low-level mind reading charm off Nadire. It got lost in the fight, so I've got no idea if he got anything from her. I didn't ask for details on what she's been thinking about for the last twenty-four hours," he says wryly and Dejan snickers around another mouthful of naan. I shake my head. So Remy does just pretend to be oblivious.

"That charm didn't do anything to her, right?" I ask. One more thing to stab Janvier for when he shows back up.

Remy shakes his head. "Probably just gave her a headache. But the gate ring got messed up." He darts an apologetic look to me like he doesn't want to blame someone. I can guess who messed it up by accident. "Can't track anything from it, but the design should help us pinpoint anything similar."

"You get a picture?" Cieran asks.

Remy chuckles wryly and indicates his fried phone. "No, but—" He shoves away some of the empty containers and presses his fingers against the table. Murmurs a few words and then pulls his hand up. Shimmering lines spread over the cleared section of table, a replica of what he saw that won't last for very long.

I stand to get a better view and snap a picture of it to upload to the laptop and better study.

"Looks Mayan." Remy's mouth tucks in a frown. He waits until I nod to end the replication spell. It fades from existence.

"Why is that bad?" Dejan asks, still dipping bits of naan in sauce and eating. He must have really overextended himself to help me earlier.

"Mostly since they used human sacrifice to fuel their blood magic."

Disgust creases Dejan's face. "But no one practices that anymore, right?"

Remy shrugs. "Empire fell centuries ago after they tried to tangle with Rome and the Iberian troops were sent over. Supposedly their magic stopped too, but who knows what got handed down verbally."

I'm running through some recognition programs. "Might not be," I say as I get a potential match.

"Better or worse?" Remy accurately reads my pursed expression.

I half-chuckle. "Well, what do you know about Mesopotamian magic?"

"They were into necromancy, right?"

We both look at Dejan who shrugs and keeps eating. "I read too, nerds."

"You can read?" Remy dodges Dejan's small shot of green-tinted magic with a smirk.

"Origins aside," Cieran cuts in. "Can you run it against any other records from cases?"

"Already on it," I reassure. "And pulling up known associates. Remy, did you get a good look at the woman who cast it?"

"Decent."

Dejan helps him start stacking empty bowls and shoving them farther down the table to make space.

I plug the laptop to a port on the table, and my view appears on a screen on the wall. "See if you recognize anyone." I start to scroll through the mug shots or surveillance photos littered through cases.

Cieran leans forward on crossed arms, jaw clenching as faces move by, including Andrej and Janvier.

"Her." Remy finally stops me. "Maybe."

"I need more than maybe, Rem," I say.

"I was a little busy," he retorts and gives me that look again.

But from what I remember in those blurred seconds of trying to stab Janvier and then getting hurled across the alley, I'm certain it's her.

It's a surveillance photo, but she's walking next to Andrej. Walking very close to Andrej.

"Great, we have a pissed off lover too?" Dejan grumbles.

Cieran leans on the table. "I don't remember her at all from intelligence or from any surveillance we did."

Photographic memory aside, I'm sure he remembers everything about the Andrej case and mission.

"If they were together, I don't know if it matters. She could still be part of whatever gang Janvier's got going right now. Police ID those other bodies?" Cieran asks.

I flip back to the police reports and messages from the lead detectives. Using the names they got, we're able to cross a few more names off the associates list.

Another chime alerts me to the search on Andrew Minnare. It's an Allied States Army record from our database. Dishonorably discharged two years ago for stealing equipment—a case of wild magic grenades, some armor with military grade protection and counter-spells etched onto it, weapons, and pre-cast wards.

Some of it showed up later in an attack run by Andrej. An attack that links to a report signed by Cieran.

One look at the ID photo and I flash back to the Wastelands mission again. To the first strike against Andrej, before he captured Cieran and Athina and gated away. To a man I killed.

The discharge is the last hit on Minnare before the data goes quiet. It doesn't take long to sort through past information before I find the name linking them both. Minnare's mother is Janvier's step-mother. She married Alan Janvier twenty years ago, died five years ago. Alan Janvier has been back in Gaul for four years.

Unease sours in my mouth. I killed Janvier's brother, and he made a point to interact with my sister and then target her café.

"Bes?" Dejan's cautious question draws my attention up. All three of them are poised on the edge of their seats, watching me, ready to go.

I swallow hard and push the ID picture to the wall display. "I killed Janvier's step-brother two months ago. Looks like he's out for revenge."

15

Besim

"He can *firren* try," Dejan says first and it's mirrored on Remy's face. They way they're both tensed, leaning toward me like they're about to protect *me* has me drawing back. Cieran looks just as determined.

"Okay, we'll put someone on the café since he's already been there. You want anyone on the rest of your family, Bes?" The practical way he asks it, has already thought it through in the milliseconds that have passed, has the same nausea rising back up. I'm still over here making some peace with the fact that it's me who's been targeted, that I haven't even followed the thought to the logical conclusion. My family could be in danger too and *I'm* the one bringing trouble.

"Besim." Cieran's sergeant voice breaks through.

I jerk my chair back like I'm about to...what? Leave?

"Bes." Remy this time, poised in his seat like he might try to jump over the table and tackle me to the ground before I do something I've never done—run from a problem.

"He's not going to touch your family." Dejan's promise is a low threat against Janvier, and there's the closest to murder I've ever seen in the medic's eyes.

I believe him, but an annoyingly practical part of my brain is saying he can't possibly promise that even if Dejan has never broken a promise, never broken trust before.

My gaze swings to Cieran, maybe hoping the sergeant will have something different for me.

"CO and I will coordinate getting your family covered. You with me, Bes?"

I jerk a nod, wrangling the sudden expansive panic back to the room and what I can control in front of me. I can't do it all. But I can trust my crew, Cieran, and whatever other team is going to be assigned to this.

"What else do we have?" he asks, and I scoot my chair to the table with an effort even though Remy and Dejan barely move, still ready to fight whatever needs to be fought. It might be my head that needs to be punched, but I'm not telling them that because they'd actually do it. Lovingly.

"There's been no hits in the last few hours since he disappeared." My voice progressively steadies over each word. "DPD had already put out watches for unauthorized gating but nothing has been triggered except for the one in the alley."

The nearest travel center with long-distance portal gates and shorter distance travel circles is fifty miles away in Portland, so we don't have to worry about closing a center in addition to monitoring the city. Portal gates and travel circles cause massive bursts of energy even non-magic wielders can sense. They're hard to hide, and it's more likely he'll be going by vehicle in any attempted getaway.

Based on how angry, and how impaled on my dirk he was, I don't think he's leaving anytime soon. No one else thinks so either based on the grim looks passed around the table.

"Okay, I'm going to go update Wolfe and start coordinating. Besim, you'll stay here or in whatever command center we set up."

All three of us treat Cieran to a "seriously" look. He can risk himself, but *I* need to be protected? He ignores us and leaves. My computer is still running programs, trying to catch any information for me, but I don't think it's going to be successful for a while. I tip it closed and make my way from the briefing room, trying not to be annoyed when neither Rem nor Dej calls after me.

———

Remy finds me twenty minutes later two floors down in the same corner nook as yesterday, laptop working on the table. I'm in the chair, rosary beads slipping between my fingers. The warlock slides down to a crouch, braced between the balls of his feet and his back against the wall. He doesn't say anything, just rests arms on his knees and waits.

I'm trying to pray. Not doing a great job since instead my mind is flicking through the events of the Wastelands, the last few days, and wildly conjuring scenarios for the foreseeable future.

I don't have much to say other than a need for everyone to be protected and safe. But past the four of us doing everything we've been trained for, that's in God's hands. I've never really had an issue trusting higher powers, but getting blown up by wild magic is apparently the thing to do it.

My hand scrubs across my forehead, and I pull another bead under my thumb. Remy will wait until I'm done. After four years, he knows what the rosary means. Sometimes asks for me to add a few things into the prayer intentions while I'm at it. Since he's here, I throw him into the mix, hoping the Blessed Mother can sort through all the jumbled mess that's this attempt and salvage something to present to the Trinity on my behalf.

I finish the last few prayers and cross myself, curling the beads into my palm. My head hangs a second longer before I look to Remy.

"You draw the short straw?"

A grin spears across his face and there's some more motion about him now that I'm done praying.

"Sarge is with the CO, and Dejan went to find some more chocolate and contact Mark to give his bag back."

Dejan needing chocolate to help stimulate magic replenishment is uncommon, and I shake my head. "He really overdid it."

Remy huffs. "Yeah, and I'm going to be lording it over him for the foreseeable future."

It gets a chuckle from me. It's not often Remy gets to flip the tables on Dejan with magic overuse, but this'll save us all from at least twenty-four hours of overdramatic sighs and aggressively long-suffering looks from the medic.

"You doing okay?" I ask. The slash on Rem's cheek has clotted and usually Dejan would have already healed something like that without being asked. The downtime and food have him looking not quite as haggard as I remember in the alley, but he's still not looking like he'll be gunning for a real fight anytime soon.

"Yeah." He flicks his hand dismissively. "Called the parents, talked to Bear. Told them I might be there for dinner, or might already be on mission."

He says it easily, but there's a faint tightening around his eyes. Leave time being unexpectedly cut short is rough, and I don't have a son I'd give the world for.

"Bear okay?"

His three-year-old son Blair is my adoptive nephew, the spitting image of Remy, and has more energy than the sun. He hasn't shown magic yet, but magic is passed through the male side of their family, and both Remy and his dad have strong fire magic from the Hawaiian Islands. It's only a matter of time before he starts to wreak even more havoc.

"He cried for two minutes before trying to bargain for me to come home." Remy shakes his head. "He's going to have a list of things we have to do together by the time I get back."

I chuckle softly. He's complaining, but he'll do every single one of them. The sobering realization that I'm the one causing this catches up and quashes the amusement.

"Sorry."

Remy tips his head back. "Why? For doing your job two months ago and doing it again today?"

See? Annoying younger brother who can occasionally say smart things. He smirks, knowing he's right and shuffling something to hold over *me* for the next twenty-four hours into his pocket.

"You get an answer?" He indicates my hand still clenched around the rosary with a flick of his finger.

Our priest once said that prayer is the closest we'll get to a landline to heaven, but the answering is on a different timetable than the call.

I shrug. "We'll see."

A knock against the wall announces Dejan. He slouches into the nearest chair and props his boots up on the arm of my chair. He's holding a half-eaten chocolate bar, but whatever he's going to say is halted as he looks at my hand.

He points in silent question. I nod and slide the rosary away. He's definitely not religious, and usually only uses the Fates to curse, but he's never hassled me about it like some other guys used to in the regular enlisted forces.

"Myerson only had fae." Dejan holds the bar in Remy's direction. The warlock declines with a grimace. He doesn't like chocolate and definitely doesn't like fae-made, especially if it's got some basic regeneration spells added in.

The elf shrugs and breaks off another piece. We sit in silence, Remy only moving to sit more comfortably on the ground and stretch his legs out. We've sat like this countless times before, but rarely in complete quiet. It's my preferred place during downtime at the tower, and fondly nicknamed "therapy corner" by more than a few guys. True to its name, I'm usually the one starting off conversations here.

But words have returned to feeling stuck inside my chest and I'm not sure how to even start breaking them far enough apart to let anything out. Remy and Dejan don't make a move to start, and I've just caught a glance they throw at each other when Cieran arrives.

"Gear up and check in with family or whoever you have. We're not going home until this is done."

16

Nadire

It's a sleepless night even after hours spent on the couch in my childhood home, drinking Mom's peppermint hot chocolate and eating way too many ginger cookies. And then staying for dinner and beating Taron at the video games I grew up playing with the older siblings.

It was subdued by Besim's text to the family. He's on mission and will be radio silent for as long as it takes. He called Mom briefly just to reassure that he was all right, but after the text it seemed like the door off the kitchen to his garage apartment loomed bigger and lonelier. Somehow worse than any other time in the last nine years of deployments and missions because he's out in the city and looking...I don't know...*fragile.*

Dad drove me home and it was a quiet ride. I teared up when he leaned over in the front seat of his truck and wrapped me in a hug.

He's the full-blooded troll, with generations of fighters in our genealogy, but he's the chill one most of the time and Mom, the human, is the one ready to scrap. It makes us laugh, Dad especially when he starts to recount in an even deeper voice the family history from when trolls were the first to walk the hills of the Norse-lands, fighting each other, Romans, dark-haired elves, Vikings, long before Christianity found them and settled the bloodlust. All while Mom stands there, arms akimbo, starting to laugh, already forgetting whatever thing she was arguing about, as he finishes "and nothing compared to you."

I want something like what they have so bad, but here I am. One coffee shop and barely furnished apartment, a dwindling savings account, inching closer and closer to defaulting on the giant loan. And so stinking tired because I couldn't sleep, remembering the explosions, the aftermath, and Besim.

I'm not technically supposed to be at the café until lunch at least, but I'm there to open. The college students who open Friday mornings just raise their eyebrows. We take turns fixing orders and puttering around cleaning tables. Or in my case, walking back and forth from the back, drinking plain coffee, straightening chairs or napkin holders, and ignoring budgets and costs and everything else.

Dad stops by again at noon, Enver with him. They're both covered in dust and mud from their site, and bright caution vests with *Antilles Construction* in block letters on the back. I roll my eyes when they come in but Dad just grins.

He's as tall as Besim, breaking six and a half feet tall. The old books and stories that paint trolls as gnarled and lopsided creatures are all wrong, and still somewhat of a sore point hundreds of years later. Trolls look human, with dull silver-grey skin like the granite stones of the far north. Bulkier jaws and thick teeth that could break rock if they really wanted to, or you know, bones like some creepy nursery rhymes say. Shoulders for days and just an aura of "don't mess with me."

Until Dad smiles and then seriously, it's like everyone in the room is grinning. Enver is the spitting image of him. He has the same stoneskin ability as Besim, so his skin coloring is the same tanned brown as Mom, but he usually keeps the stoneskin active around sites. Astrid has light grey skin that shimmers in direct sun. Lars's skin is a marbled effect of stoneskin and human skin. It's patterned around something called a dermatome which means his body developed it around spinal nerve connections. It looks pretty cool, and having older brothers like Enver and Besim meant he was never given crap about it from anyone outside the family growing up.

"Just came to check on you," Dad says.

"Dad, I'm not five." But I definitely take the hug and get one from Enver too.

"Dad told me I had to come," Enver says like he's not thirty-two.

I jab my elbow into his ribs and convince them to try Maya's new drink. She's in for the afternoon, and gets introduced and checked on once Dad learns she was here when the explosions happened.

They don't stay long, and once their comforting presence leaves, I'm back to puttering around until Maya glares at me for rearranging the peppermint jar *again*.

But I don't leave, other than to step outside and watch the police tape still flutter in the winter breeze. A few people pause on the outskirts of it, shaking their heads before hurrying on. Two policemen are positioned around, keeping watch, making sure no one lingers very long.

Cieran stops by once to talk to them. He's in full uniform, sword buckled on, and hands hooked into his armored vest. And it's not the wind making me shudder. I lean against the brick exterior, arms crossed and trying to bury myself in my faded sweatshirt.

I'm looking at my sneakers, trying to think about literally anything else, when a soft, "Hey," brings my attention up.

It's Cieran and he definitely looks like a sergeant today. "Doing okay?" he asks, hands still hooked in his vest.

I nod, scrubbing hands up and down my arms. "It's just been slow today, 'cause of..." I jerk my thumb at the destruction two blocks up the street.

"But are *you* doing okay?"

A faint smile tugs, and I reply, "You been taking lessons from my brother?"

Cieran chuckles, but it doesn't really alleviate the tightness hovering around him. "I know what avoiding thinking about things looks like."

His words somehow reassure and I straighten. "I'm okay. Just maybe not built for stuff like this."

His chuckle comes with a wry tilt of the head. "Not many people are." His focus slides to my left as he reaches up to his ear and taps. "Got it."

"Is Besim okay?" I ask before he can pivot away.

He reaches up to his ear again. "Besim, your sister wants to know if you're okay." It's said with a straight face, but whatever my brother says back has him chuckling.

"He and Dejan got short straw this morning," Cieran explains and I'm reasonably sure I don't want to know what that means. "He's fine."

I raise an eyebrow and he acknowledges. "Let us know if you see anything," he says and then is gone, striding easily away.

I watch the empty street for another long minute until a flurry of snow drifts in front of my face and I retreat inside. The rest of the afternoon passes painfully slow, but I can't quite bring myself to kick out the few people who dared to come out today and just close up. Maya's behind the counter, textbooks spread out around her. I take myself up to the high-top and pull out my phone.

Trying to keep planning the sibling dinner seems pointless and a little dangerous, knowing Besim is on duty. Like it might jinx something. So

I set it screen down and rest my forehead against my hands, blowing out a sigh.

"Hey." Maya hops up into the chair across from me. "You want to talk about it?"

"You have to study. Don't you have tests coming up?" I return.

"Yeah, but this seems more important." She shrugs, and it makes me slide my arms forward onto the table, halfway draped across it. Maya smiles, and gestures for me to start talking.

So I do, and give the quiet recap of what happened yesterday when I ran out the door. She's leaning on the table as I finish, brow pinched.

"That's intense."

"Yeah." I pull back, propping on elbows. "And it just felt like a lot, but compared to Bes and the guys—"

"Hey." She reaches over and taps my arm. "Don't compare. Firstly, because you're not some insane spec-ops guy whose job it is to protect people."

"You don't have to be so logical about it," I retort, and the tiny blue butterfly clips in her curls shift their wings with her chuckle.

"And I don't think you should feel bad at all that you're shaken up."

I crack a smile and a bit of tension chips away. Like I needed someone's validation first before I could start to process.

Hours keep inching by, but I don't give up and go home. Mostly because my apartment is quiet, and I'd rather meander around and at least have the odd chance at conversation to keep putting off some of the flashbacks.

Nothing from Besim, not that I expected there to be, but it's odd knowing he's on duty here in Dunhare instead of some far-off place.

Family checks in throughout the day. Even the siblings who don't normally text send something.

Finally eight p.m. rolls around and I call it. Maya has gotten more studying done today than she ever has. I feel bad, but I also don't want to rob her of the chance at a paycheck. She's putting away her apron in the back as I lock the front door. I straighten a few chairs as I head to check the tablet and be depressed over low sales one more time before logging out.

The bell jingles behind me, and I frown, turning to tell whoever it is that we're closed. Stopping when I remember *I definitely locked it.*

And standing there in the door, woman behind him, is Damien Janvier.

"Hello, Nadire." Gone is the charm, and there's a sort of bared-teeth anger to him. His left arm is bound up in a sling and as he moves forward, I backpedal. I'd given Bes crap about labeling him a terrorist yesterday, but I see it now.

"What..." It comes out a bare whisper. "What do you want?"

His chiseled features sharpen into a feral smile, and the woman behind him has the same bone-chilling expression as she raises her hand. The lights flicker, and the door locking by her power is audible in the shocking silence.

"Your brother killed my brother two months ago and then stabbed me. Consider this the bonus to my revenge."

The counter arrests my movement and I brace against it. A soft, panicked, "Nadire?" has me twisting and my heart falling even further. Maya comes slowly from the back, hands raised, as a bulky man prods her along. Her wide eyes beg me for an explanation. But I've got nothing.

"Back's locked down, boss," the man says. Damien snags a chair, flipping it around and sinking into it. One leg hooks over the other knee and he leans back. The woman standing next to him holds her right hand out from her side, flickering shadows swirling all around.

I didn't even need the threat of magic to be paralyzed.

"I...I don't know where Besim is." It squeaks out.

"Oh." Damien clicks his tongue. "You have a phone, don't you?"

"He's off-grid, looking..."

"For me?" Damien smiles again and I'm honestly embarrassed I ever considered him attractive. "Let's help him out, shall we? It's what a good sibling would do."

A good sibling would do a lot of things, and luring a brother into a terrorist trap is nowhere on that list.

He raises an eyebrow, sending a pointed look at me. "Phone."

"Nadi." Maya's cautious voice pauses my hand as I reach to my back pocket. She shakes her head slightly. *Don't do it.* But the man behind her pulls a knife and I can see the slight way she flinches, braces against just the sound. It's like she's been in some similar situation but obviously I can't ask, and can't let her get hurt either.

Guess it's a good thing I'm about to call my special forces brother who is definitely more than just a Communications Specialist. I hope he brings his longsword and finishes the job this time.

I muster a small smile that lacks any confidence, and Maya just gives a tiny nod back. I'm not really sure what it means, and I'm hoping it's not a "ride and/or definitely be about to die if you don't figure something out."

"Phone," Damien snaps, and my shaky fingers unlock the phone and pull up Besim's contact. I'm torn between hoping his phone is off and praying he'll answer.

"Speaker," comes the next order and for a few seconds all we hear is the droning ring.

My heart stops with the small *click* of connection and his deep voice answering, "Nadi, this isn't a good time."

17

Besim

A day of nothing finishes with us back in Wolfe's office, reporting. The other two crews are still out in the city, sending updates through comms. CO even pulled in Ylan's deep cover team for extra surveillance around whatever it is they're doing. We haven't heard from them yet, so they've also got nothing.

"All right, go get some food over in mess. They should know you're coming in," Wolfe says.

Remy's boots scuff the carpet. None of us are thrilled to be eating mess hall food when we could be eating whatever he'd make instead.

Wolfe catches the motion, and chuckles. "I don't need a war on my base, Kalama."

Remy offers a tired smile. "Yes, sir."

Today's been nothing but protein bars and canteens of water snagged around small breaks, so honestly, anything that's not that will be fine with me.

Wolfe's desk phone rings and he answers, lifting his hand to wave us out in dismissal, then closing his fist tight in signal to hold. The air shifts as we settle back, ready for whatever news is on the other end of the phone. But if it's mission related, it'd be coming through the comms, so the uncertainty is palpable.

"Okay, it's clear. I'll send him down." He clicks the phone back to the receiver. "Sergeant, head down to the lobby, there's something for you."

But Cieran doesn't relax until Wolfe makes a shooing motion. We're right behind Cieran, unspoken, unasked for support for whatever's down there.

He's first into the lobby from the stairs, hand gripping his sword, but coming up short.

"Athina?"

The other half of his heartbond stands in the lobby, and we're just as confused because Athina Spera is supposed to be thousands of miles away in her own country. But here she is, knee-length jacket barely covering up her old-style breastplate harness, short sword strapped to her waist, and heavy knee-high boots over fitted black military pants.

She drops the duffel bag over her shoulder and strides to meet Cieran, both pulling each other into a ferocious hug like they're the only thing that'll keep the other standing.

Small motion beside me has me glancing to Dejan. The elf watches them, an odd set to his jaw, something *sad* flickering before it's shuttered away.

"What are you doing here?" Cieran asks, pulling away slightly.

Her hand rests on his chest over the tac vest and chain mail. "You needed me." Her common has a tumbling cadence, voice used to the dragonwalker language of the Kirnae Archipelago.

But Cieran shakes his head, leaning away. "No, I'll figure this out." He jabs a thumb at his head. "It's just the same shit to get through."

"Cieran," she interrupts softly, this time pressing a hand to his cheek. "You needed me."

His posture collapses. "Yeah." The word comes broken.

She pulls the bond dampener off his wrist and his arms circle her again, a breath escaping as his forehead rests on her shoulder. She presses the side of her head against his, likely slipping to the mindspeak they can now share with the dampeners off.

It's a moment we shouldn't be watching, but we are, and it's stabbing something through my heart. Like I needed the visual that it's okay to lean on someone else, it's okay that someone can look out for you. I tilt a guilty look at Dejan and Remy. But before I can say anything, my phone buzzes.

It's Nadire. I almost slide it away before the remembrance of me telling her to call if anything happens. She knows I'm on mission and not to call...but...

I hit answer. "Nadi, this isn't a good time."

"Bes." Her voice comes breathless. Scared.

"What's going on?" I ask, and immediately feel Remy and Dejan's attention lock on to me.

"Um...I know you're busy..."

"Nadi." It comes short. "Where are you?"

"Coffee shop. Maya's here too." Definitely scared.

"Anyone else with you?" I look up and find Cieran joining the loose circle around me, Athina at his shoulder, her razor-sharp focus on me as well, ready to go.

"Yes." It's short, also odd if I hadn't already been on high alert. "Can you come over?"

I tuck my phone between my shoulder and ear, and pull my tablet out of the front pocket of my vest. I wirelessly connect the tablet to the phone and start a GPS locator. Remy settles a hand around one of his knives, lifting his chin in silent question. He can track anything, with or without magic assist, but needs something belonging to the person to feed into a tracker spell. I don't have anything of Nadi's on me, but I do share blood with her.

"If Janvier can hold a phone with that arm of his, put him on." It's a gamble, but one I'm sure of. There's no other reason she would be calling me scared.

A quick gasp of fear crackles across the line, and then a male voice takes over.

"Besim Antilles, is it?" Janvier's got a deeper tone, and it's rife with the promises of violence if he doesn't get his way.

Tablet shows the signal is coming from Nadi's café, and Remy's waiting on my go-ahead to start a different kind of tracker to follow Nadi wherever she goes. My hand clenches. Wait.

"What do you want?"

"I'll keep this simple. Good old-fashioned revenge," he says. "You killed my brother in the Wastelands two months ago. He was one of the best things this world had to offer."

Minnare's burgeoning rap sheet begs to differ, but apparently Janvier and I have fierce loyalty to siblings as common ground.

"You also tried to ruin my arm. I want to return the favor before I kill you. You have fifteen minutes to get over here, alone, or I start taking it out on your sister."

My hand clenches around my phone, threatening to crush it. Remy and Dejan have hands on weapons and Cieran's on his phone, murmuring something before hanging up.

"We can keep this easy," I return through tight jaw. "Turn yourself in and you'll live to see tomorrow."

"Oh," he tuts. "You forget I've got the leverage here. And I know you understand the pain of seeing a sibling suffer."

My gut twists as I hear a surprised exclamation from Nadire.

"Don't you *faen* dare," I growl.

"Fifteen minutes." The line clicks dead.

It takes me a second to lower the phone, hands shaking. Those who don't know me well always joke that I probably didn't get the old troll traits because they only see the easy-going, calm side. But it's there, and it's about to come out because someone threatened my family.

A door slams and Wolfe strides over to meet us, brow drawn in concern.

"Bes." Cieran speaks first. His hands are hooked in the collar of his vest, feet braced wider, ready to move as soon as I report.

"Janvier has Nadi at her café. I've got fifteen minutes to get over there—alone—or he goes after her."

Dejan snorts at the "alone," and a bit of heat ramps up around Remy. It's ten minutes at least to the café, but at this hour the roads will be clear and that area has had low traffic all day due to the attack, so should be an easier in.

"On you, Sergeant," Wolfe defers.

"Okay. I'll radio Cox's team to set up a perimeter. We'll cover inside. Sure you want to go in?" Cieran asks me.

I return his even stare. "That's my sister in there."

"Exactly. I need an even head."

I shove the tablet away and pocket my phone. "Don't worry about me, Sergeant."

His eyebrow lifts. Athina softly clears her throat and pulls our attention. Her eyes are a dark brown, tinged with a bit of copper. The same color highlights her dark hair, braided around her head. But the sight of those eyes brings back the thought of another pair of dark eyes filled with laughter while hiding something inside.

"Maya's there too. Employee," I clarify for Wolfe.

A soft curse escapes Cieran. "Just the two of them?"

"That's all Nadi gave me."

"She didn't happen to say how many combatants?"

I shake my head. Nadi's not trained in any form of combat or reconnaissance except the type that comes naturally with being a younger sister.

"Okay. Who else can we pull in?" Cieran asks Wolfe.

Our CO pulls out his phone. "Crew Nine is on duty here. They'll gear up and join Cox on setting up a perimeter. You four will be close-quarters. Cox will be backup. I can pull Ylan's team."

But Cieran shakes his head. "Getting them involved might blow their cover. Three teams should be fine. You'll coordinate with DPD?"

Wolfe affirms, and checks his watch. We've already wasted two minutes with this. Athina shucks her jacket, revealing more knives and more armor. Cieran pivots to take her in, and Wolfe crosses his arms.

"Spera."

"Commander," she returns as she tightens the bracer on her right forearm.

"Where do you think you're going?"

We all pause, but she doesn't back down. Doesn't even seem phased by the question.

"I know I am not part of your army, Commander, but I have fought alongside your men, am heartbonded to one, and I hear two women are trapped by a terrorist. Besides"—she flashes a dangerous smile, further highlighted by the sudden sharpness to her incisors—"I can bring a real dragon to your Drax soldiers."

Wolfe sighs, a faint smile threatening his stern features. "We still haven't reached any agreement on what a partnership looks like between our two countries."

Athina hums, and her features ease back to pure human, no threat of a fifty foot, red-scaled dragon imminent. "Then consider this a step towards coordination."

Wolfe actually chuckles this time. "The law heads won't be happy."

"They never are," Athina says. Wolfe laughs and looks to us but we all shrug. We've fought next to her and have zero issues with her coming along. And Cieran definitely doesn't. He looks to her and something like a blush finally hits her dark brown skin at whatever he says through the mindspeak.

"Remy, get us some wheels. I'll get you a comm set," Cieran tells Athina. "Out front in two."

He grabs her bag and jacket to drop off with our quartermaster, and he and Remy break into a run. Dejan, Athina, and I head outside to wait.

Remy's not proficient enough in gates to open one and instantly transport us to the café. Something about fire magic doesn't lend itself well to gating, and he's come close to overdrawing his reserves the times he's had to. Gating comes more effortlessly to earth- and air-based magic. Rem's is specialized more for combat, and even if he did gate, it'd just alert Janvier we were coming. We've got slightly more chance to sneak up and avoid triggering any more magic traps in a vehicle, but I can hear the ticking clock with each passing second.

But Remy's fast, and he's got a Humvee around in two minutes just as Cieran joins us, breathless and holding a comm set. We pile in, Cieran helping Athina with the comms in the back. I'm in front, and Remy floors it.

18

Besim

I have ten seconds to spare as I walk into the café. From the outside, it looks like normal. Bright lights shine through lowered shades over the broad windows, a few figures silhouetted at tables.

The low murmurs of my crew setting into place hum in my ear as the bell dings and the door swings slowly closed behind me.

Nadi's my first priority. She stands, compressed over crossed arms, at the counter, Janvier beside her. Her wide eyes meet mine, and she nods her head slightly. She's okay for now.

"Watch your step, there's wards everywhere," Dejan's voice crackles.

"Already on it," Remy replies before Cieran can check in.

"You alone?" Janvier asks, a snap of green-tinted magic appearing around his good hand.

I spread my arms in answer.

He smiles thinly. "I'd like a verbalization."

"Scared?" I ask, sweeping a glance around, making three more men. And Maya in a chair by the back wall, under hovering guard. She gives the same tight nod at my look. Unlike my sister, she's sitting taller, eyes not as wide, looking like she's ready to jump someone when given the signal. A small camera on my vest feeds into my tablet outside in Cieran's hand, giving him the information.

"Indulge me." The magic-coated hand sweeps toward Nadi, and my confident sister moves her head slightly, like she's cringing away.

"Did you bring my knife back?" I don't indulge him, giving my team some more time to get in position.

Janvier smiles thinly and inches his hand closer to Nadire. I lurch forward a step, halted by his warning. A soft noise escapes Nadi as his magic crackles and snaps, trying to latch on to her through the bare space between the spell and her face.

"Does she have the stoneskin like you do?" Janvier casually asks.

"In position." All four are set. And I hope Nadi will forgive me when her café inevitably gets torn to pieces as soon as I give the signal.

But I never get the chance. I'm already drawing my longsword in response to the threat I feel creeping up behind me, even as Maya leans forward and shouts, "Watch out!"

I get a quarter turn around before heat slams into me and I'm shoved back a few paces. The urge to curl up, recoil from the fire is barely kept in check by Nadi's scream. There's no flame, no burning, just the female sorcerer from the alley standing there, the same furious intensity about her as she crushes another amulet between her hands and spreads them wide, some sort of crackling electric spell rising.

And she's focused on me.

I shout "Go!" through the comm and charge her. I've got no counter-wards, no warlock behind me to throw up a shield or take her on, just me hopefully surprising her with actually racing towards whatever she's spinning instead of trying to run.

I grab a wooden chair with one hand—I'm not about to attack her with anything metal—and swing it one-handed. She's forced to jump back and loses hand positioning, disrupting the spell for a precious second. Enough for me to swing my longsword.

My shoulder is wrenched a second time in twenty-four hours, blade knocked off course by a blast of green magic. Janvier leans forward, rage in his eyes as he keeps me from skewering his girlfriend.

And then everything erupts.

Remy's first in, magic coiling around his arms as he slams through the front door, immediately engaging the woman. The man closest to the back shouts and tumbles over a table, away from a purposeful Athina. Dejan's right behind her, and Cieran's "Bes, go," behind me announces we're all in.

I leave him and Rem to deal with Janvier and the woman, and head straight for Nadi, who's standing in shock by the counter, mouth open in horror at Dejan and Athina taking on the other two men. I grab her arm and she at least tries to reflexively punch me as I hustle her around the counter.

"Bes!" She's one decibel shy of a scream.

"Move!" I instruct, and jerk my head in an invitation for Maya to join us from the corner she found as soon as Athina appeared.

Remy shouts and everything quiets. I spin, placing the women behind me, sweeping sword up at the ready. A shimmering green field walls Janvier and the woman off from us and the rest of the room. The two goons on our side had the good sense to just surrender, and they're kneeling at sword point.

Remy and Cieran are poised mere steps from the shield. The woman smiles that same unsettling smile, and her eyes go completely black as she spreads her hands, darkness coiling all around before she rips off a necklace threaded with small amulets and hurls it to the ground.

Both she and Janvier are grinning, and it's an eerie, teeth bared, exultant look. Her hands rise again, and the coiling smoke hits the shattered amulets.

"Bad news." Remy backs away, drawing his basalt sword. "I think that gate circle was Mesopotamian."

"Oh shit." Dejan says what we're all thinking, judging by the way everyone in the room retreats a step.

"Yeah." Remy sets his feet wider, dropping into a slight crouch to anchor his magic, left hand opening in warning.

"Besim…" A whimper comes from behind me and Nadi's hand clamps around my shoulder.

"You might be about to see dead people." I watch in the same horrified fascination as everyone else, even the goons.

Shadowy figures rise, twisting, jerking to feet and shaking out limbs. Eight total and as the smoke streams away, it leaves no doubt that they're officially undead. Armor is dusty and war-torn, skin grey and flaking, caught somewhere between decomposed and restored. The café reeks of death, rusted iron, and spells gone wrong. The sorceress lists to the side, face pale and eyes bleeding smoke, as her body rejects the amount of dark magic she just did.

But Janvier pushes a green-tinged hand to her chest and she rights herself in seconds. Some healing spell using his natural magic.

"You'll be added to the collection." Janvier jabs a hand at Cieran. "Payment for killing Andrej."

Athina growls and starts toward him, but checks herself, maybe in response to Cieran, who's not looking too perturbed at the possibility of becoming an undead.

"Well then, let's get this party started." Cieran sweeps his sword up into guard position, setting his shield in place.

The eight undead warriors, all in different armors from different time periods, rattle their weapons. Two from the ancient days of the Roman Empire stand next to a sixth century centurion. Another from the Middle Centuries readies sword alongside a burly fighter from some forgotten Germanic tribe. There's a slender warrior from the Mesopotamian culture the sorceress stole the practice from. The last two wear more modern kit—from the Second World War, and the other with a Russian armed forces patch on his tac vest.

They've been busy robbing graves all over the place.

Janvier twists his wrist and shoves his clenched hand forward. Remy's basalt sword flares red as he sweeps it up parallel, bracing the flat of the blade against the back of his raised left forearm to aid his counter-spell. Janvier's spell bends and warps over Remy and Cieran, trying to suppress them until pure wild magic, deep blue and hotter than a bonfire, rolls off Remy.

He braces in a deeper crouch, then slams his forearms together, sword angled forward. He stomps his right foot down, each motion coming with a sharp word in Hawaiian and directing his counter-spell. It latches into Janvier's magic and then with a jaw-clenched cry, Remy slams his foot down, hits his chest with a left fist before shoving his hand forward, palm out, and slashes through air with his basalt sword.

Flame roars eagerly, the basalt glowing red as it's fed with wildfire channeled from Remy's center. Janvier's thrown backward under the sheer force of it.

It's been a while since I've seen Remy use that much magic, that precisely. There's barely singe marks on the ground, and he's still standing, chest heaving, but still steady on his feet. He'd already been prepping the counter-spell while the dead were being raised.

Everyone but the undead are in awe of what he just did. The soldiers charge and weapons clash. The Russian jumps the counter, knocking stacks of paper cups and the tablet register as he does, not even batting his undead eyes. I shove Nadi farther behind me, and thrust. He blocks, but I'm still moving forward, catching his blade against the slight flare in mine, trapping it long enough to get up close and smash the pommel into his face.

His head snaps back, and then rebounds with a hole where I'd hit, and not a care that I'd just opened his head up.

No blood, and coming right back for me.

19
Besim

"Get outside," I yell over my shoulder.

A flash of red alerts me to the Roman centurion coming at my right side, gladius in hand and no mercy in his glassy eyes.

The scrambling behind me is Nadire and Maya obeying, through the short hallway and exiting the back door. The metal door slams against the outer bricks, and then we're out in the late night and dull glower of the light just above the frame.

A rumble shakes the ground beneath our feet and glass shatters inside. A muted wail comes from Nadi in response, but I've got two undead coming at me. We're in a wide alley and the Roman's trying to get around at the women. He's fast, the Russian maybe slowed due to the hole in his head, and I've got my work cut out for me.

Longswords aren't made for alleys, and the Roman gets up under my sword, stabbing with his gladius. I twist and it lodges into my armored vest instead. He yanks to free it, and I stumble with it, pulling a dagger as I come and stabbing into his neck. He doesn't flinch, still trying to get his sword back.

A scream breaks my concentration and Nadi's "*Besim!*" redoubles my efforts. I lunge backward, and our joint counterpull frees the sword from my armor. As the undead staggers back, I sweep with my longsword, beheading him. The body crumples, disintegrating as it goes.

The Russian had gone around me once distracted and is closing in on the women. Maya has a flickering shield of grey-tinted magic and behind her, Nadi hurls brick shards or random garbage, but he is single-minded in his attack. They're doing their best to duck and dodge away from his strikes, but he's going to get lucky soon. One lurching step forward and I grab the back of his collar, yanking him off-balance and spinning him away from them.

He keeps his feet, and comes back swinging. I retreat a few steps, bringing him farther from Nadi and Maya, but can't spare them much of a glance. Something flies out of the café door, and Dejan gets up, swiping blood from his mouth, murderous look on his face as a second Roman leaps forward to attack.

"Head shot!" Dejan yells, trying to get the undead backed up against the wall.

"Already got it," I return, getting close enough to smash the Russian's face again. He's slowing, but still coming, finally faltering enough for me to finish him off with a swipe.

I take a step to help Dejan when a roar of fire erupts to my right. I flinch away, but lock on to a figure trapped inside the burning circle. Nadi presses against the wall, mouth open in wordless horror before she looks to me, which means...Maya.

The half-fae hunches in the circle, shielding her head, flames trying to eat at her. Remy is still inside. No one to deal with the sprung ward-trap. My heart pounds and I feel lightheaded at the sight of the wildfire. A muted cry pushes me forward before I can think, and I bull through the flames, catching Maya between my arms and pushing us both out. Her foot tangles between mine and we fall. I'm barely able to twist so she lands on me, instead of me crushing her to the pavement.

Her head thuds into my shoulder, further knocking the breath from me.

"You okay?" I wheeze, craning my head up to make sure the fire didn't attach to any clothes and follow us out.

Maya scrambles up, tearing out of my arms still locked around her, nearly punching me in the face as she does. And then she's staring at me, looking shaken for the first time tonight. I roll to my knees, and gently press hands to her shoulders.

"You okay?" I repeat.

She nods numbly. "Yeah, I have some minor wards in place." Her voice shakes and then she's turning to Nadi as my sister crashes next to us.

The sorceress flies through the door, flinging some spell over her shoulder as the world war era soldier covers. Remy appears, only to get thrown sideways under the impact. One of the living minions rushes out to protect the sorceress. Dejan's dealt with the Roman and squares up with the new threat.

Remy landed two feet from me, and moves sluggishly. In the lamplight and the fading trap fire, his face strains as his hand clenches around something on his chest. One of the undead turns his way and I jolt to my feet, swiping sword through its throat before it quite registers me. It disintegrates, and I risk a glance down.

Remy's head thuds back against the ground, and he half-shouts something before ripping his hand away and smashing the contained spell against the ground. Noxious red smoke puffs up and dissipates just as quickly.

Maya reaches toward him, gentle pale light around her hand. But Remy lurches away, short sword poised in threat.

"Don't touch me." The gritted words hold an edge of panic. Maya leans back, and the magic fades as she spreads her hands wide. Remy's breath comes uneven before recognition sets in, and apology forms in its place. But I don't have time to question the response I've never seen before.

Athina's chased out the tribal undead, and then Janvier's booking it out of the door. Cieran joins the fray, stalking into the alley, shield smoking and sword darkened from undead dust.

I haul Remy to his feet, and glance over my shoulder at the women. Maya raises her ward shield again and Nadi clutches half a brick in one hand, the other in a fist. She packs a solid punch if she means it and looks frantic enough to hit the next thing that moves.

"Stay back," I say.

We don't even make sure they acknowledge before stepping back into the fray. The ground tremors again and the sorceress makes a grabbing motion, tearing chunks of brick from the opposite building and then throwing them forward. Shards of brick fly, and Remy and I twist, trying to duck in time. He gets a barrier up, but some sneak by and a tearing sensation opens my cheek and dampness dribbles down.

Still no stoneskin.

Remy drops the shield and moves like he's going to reach out to me, but I face off with the alley again, ignoring the stinging in my shoulder that means I got hit there again.

Cieran crouches a few feet from the sorceress, shield up to block the debris. She's not doing so great either, maybe finally hitting the dregs of her stolen and innate power. Cieran stiffens and then takes a step toward her, bracing his shield with both arms. Athina appears behind him at a run, grabs the shield to support her upper body and swings into a kick that takes the sorceress across the face and throws her to the ground.

She's down, but the four remaining undead are not. Cieran and Athina are shoulder to shoulder to now, and Janvier looks pissed. He's spinning something new, both arms spread even though the heavily bandaged one is wobbling. Remy lurches forward, blue magic rippling, trying to predict whatever he's going to throw.

Dejan beheads the world war soldier, and I'm moving before I even open my mouth to warn him about the tribal undead swinging an axe behind him.

Dejan whirls, sword poised at the movement behind him, eyes widening as the undead disintegrates and I'm standing there instead. Before he can say anything, a concussive blast catches us both and slams us sideways into the wall. Weapons clatter away, shaken loose from our hands. My vision blurs red and the alley tilts, bringing some nausea with it.

I shakily push into sitting, the world wobbling like we've put out to sea. Dejan sprawls beside me, unmoving. Blue light winks out. Remy's down. Cieran and Athina fight off new attackers. I blink, trying to make sense of it. There's too many. The undead should be sent to eternal rest.

Louder sound has my head tilting the opposite direction. A crouched figure is shouting my name, pointing to something. I dumbly track Janvier stalking forward, the steel blade in his hand catching every bit of light.

Dejan's elbows buckle as he tries to get up, hindered further by a quick flash of magic from Janvier that sends him crumpling with a strained cry. Janvier and I stare at each other for a moment. His gaze flicks back to

Dejan and he swings his blade overhead, ready to slam down on Dejan's neck.

It's like I can hear the whistle of the steel parting air molecules on its way down, and some sound tears from me in response. I jolt sideways and throw up a hand, fingers wide to catch it.

It's too late to pull away, grab a knife instead. I'm frozen, watching helplessly as the sword swings down toward my bare hand because I forgot for a second that my stoneskin isn't working. But at least Dejan's not going to be killed yet.

Shouts and frantic motion speeds up around us and the sword impacts.

20

Besim

My arm jolts down before I stop the momentum with the force of my muscles pushing back. Both Janvier and I stare in shock at the silver sheen coating my hand. My stone-coated fingers close around the blade before he can pull away.

I yank forward, barely enough room for the motion to knock him off-balance before the sword point hits the wall behind me. He staggers and I twist further, tucking my knee up to my chest before kicking his leg out from under him. Janvier spins to the ground, and this time is unable to stop my knife coming for his heart.

Other figures rush in and Janvier's body is pulled away, leaving his sword still wobbling in my grasp. It takes another blink to realize Cox's team has arrived from the perimeter, and is taking care of the reinforcements that came from somewhere.

"Bes!" Dejan grabs my sleeve, about as pale as I feel. I drop the sword and a strangled breath escapes.

"Bes!" Remy hits his knees in front of us, magic-coated hand reaching out like he's going to help somehow. And this time, I don't recoil from the threat of wildfire.

"Shit." Dejan's head thuds against my shoulder in relief.

"Ow," I groan, the action pulling at the injuries sustained before my stoneskin decided to reappear.

I lift my shaking hand, watching the silver fade back to tanned skin that's bloody and dirt-streaked. And call it up again. It responds, bringing with it the light tingle of stone rippling over my skin to protect. I can feel it rushing up my arm under the chain mail, gamely shoving through the burn scarring, though it's thinner there in some way I can't explain, only feel. It halts at my shoulder, but that's okay for now.

My entire body feels more alive than it has in weeks, remembering the gift that's been suppressed since I got hit by the wild magic in the Wastelands.

Remy's hand drops on my other shoulder, and Dejan's fist pushes against my chest.

"You *firren* idiot!" But a strangled laugh comes from the elf. A smile cracks Remy's exhausted face, and I tip my head back against the rough brick with a bewildered laugh.

The warlock stands and extends a hand down. I take it, and slowly get to my feet.

"Bes!" Nadi barges in, halting just shy of hugging me. Her face is pale but she appears to be in one piece. I open my arms and get knocked back a half step as she throws her arms around me.

"You okay?" I murmur against her head, holding her just as tight.

"Yeah. Are you?"

I'm a lot of things right now, and some of it is too confusing to sort through just yet. "I'll be okay."

Her sniff is accompanied by a shaking through her shoulders.

"You're okay." It's about all I can give right now. Maya's a few steps away, Athina poised next to her, sharp eyes assessing both women. Cox's team has taken charge, getting the newcomers and the sorceress cuffed. Janvier isn't moving and the way he's twisted on the ground with a knife in his heart announces he's not getting back up.

Remy gets Dej on his feet, and the elf lists slightly. Cieran limps over as Nadi starts to peel herself away.

"Everyone good?" he asks.

We all give some form of affirmation, Remy with a wince. He looks to Nadire and asks, "You don't happen to have any chocolate around, do you?"

"What?" Her confusion takes up her entire face.

He waves his hand, pointing to himself. "Magic."

"Oh." Understanding fills her voice. "Inside." But she balks as she turns to face the back door.

"Hold up." Cieran extends a hand before tapping it to his ear. "Everything clear inside?" Then he nods. "Okay, Crew Nine just cleared it. Let's head in for a few minutes. I'll need some reports before we go anywhere."

Despite the reassurance, Nadire still hesitates, until I nudge her shoulder and lead the way in.

It's a mess and I turn to apologize, halting at the miserable look on her face. The street facing windows are shattered, glass everywhere on the floor. At least one table is in pieces on the ground, the others shoved or overturned in the fray. A few chairs have been tossed together, legs tangled up. The service counter is pretty well swiped clear of anything. Maya picks her way behind Nadi to right the espresso machine with one end hanging perilously off the edge.

"Oh," is all that escapes my sister.

"The windows were my fault," Remy sheepishly says. "I'm really sorry."

Nadire offers a wavering smile. "Since all of you *insane* guys just saved my life, I can probably forgive some windows. And I'm paying enough for insurance, they'd better cover all this." And then, like the words bolster her, she moves behind the counter, picking up the cracked tablet and setting it on the counter, before digging in a drawer.

She hands Remy a chocolate bar. "Private reserve," she says.

"Thanks." He lifts the bar. "I'll help clean up in a bit."

Nadire waves him off. "I don't really want to think about it right now." Again comes the rueful smile. "Just go sit down. All of you guys look awful."

But we don't make a move just yet.

Dejan limps closer. "Either of you hurt at all?" There's a gentle edge to him again, and it's almost bewildering to see.

"No," comes their answers though Maya seems to be giving Remy a wide berth. He notices, for once picking up on a signal from a woman, and focuses on her.

"Sorry about before." If I didn't know him better, I'd think he's stammering. "You just caught me off guard."

A small smile edges across Maya's lips and something about the sight relieves me more than I want to admit. "It's okay. I came right up on you, didn't I?" She rubs her arms. "And I don't really use my magic anyway, so probably wouldn't have helped."

An awkward nod passes between them, and they both seem relieved to put more space between each other.

"Bes," Nadire says warningly as I look to her again. "Go sit down."

For once, I don't mind obeying a younger sibling, and stumble my way over to the nearest bench shoved up against the wall. Dejan collapses next to me, and Remy sinks down to the ground with a groan, picking at the chocolate bar once he's settled.

Cieran slides up onto the counter a few feet away, like he's not sure if he's welcome with us. Athina touches his shoulder, distracting him before any of us can drag him over.

"That was a pretty cool move." He flashes a tired smile up at her.

She beams back, and steps in front of him, pulling him into a hug. He rests his head on her shoulder, arms looping around her.

"Don't you dare start making out or I'm gonna throw up," Dejan calls and the two of them flip him off, Cieran without lifting his head. Remy chuckles, breaking a piece off the bar, grimacing as he starts to eat.

"I don't understand you." Dejan leans forward, beckoning until Remy extends the bar and the elf snaps off a piece. I wave off the offer, preferring to slouch against the wall and let it hold me up.

"You doing okay, Bes?" Dejan's fist taps my knee. Remy casts a side-long glance up.

I sigh and finally say it out loud. "Haven't been for awhile."

"*Finally.*" Dejan's response takes me off guard.

"What?" I stare at him.

"Everyone's been mad at us for weeks," Remy says. "They think we're not taking care of you."

The only thing I seem capable of is staring.

"Emma was yelling at me the other day," Dejan says. "You know how terrifying it is to get lectured by a dwarf?"

"Yes," Remy and I both automatically respond. Quartermaster Emma Myerson doesn't mince words, and you'd best not destroy her gear without some really good explanation. Heaven help you if she puts on her glasses.

"You...?" Somehow I'm still confused.

"You haven't been okay since waking up in the hospital." Remy jabs the chocolate at me.

"And for once, you're not *firren talking*." Dejan's elbow prods my side. "I'm offended he doesn't think we noticed," he says to Remy.

"Have you met you?" Remy says, jerking his feet out of the way of Dejan's stomp.

A faint laugh escapes me, bringing with it a mix of relief and embarrassment that I haven't realized how much they've been around—at the hospital, at the command tower, on off-duty days for them when I was still on medical leave. Either one or both, talking or not talking, being their usual selves around me, trying to get me out of the place I've been stuck since getting hit.

"Sorry," I say. "I just..." They patiently wait for me to finally get it all out. And I know I have to.

"Felt invincible until you weren't?" Cieran's voice draws my gaze up to the sergeant standing there, hands hooked in his armored vest. He's also been around a bit, sticking to my side even though he hasn't decided what he's going to do.

"Yeah." I nod. "I've never felt that helpless before, and it made me...scared." It sounds so simple, so basic. Childish. But no one's laughing or judging. "I can grab a sword"—I flex my hand, feeling the bone-deep reverberations of the steel against stone—"but that magic ate right through me." The last words come out a whisper and I can't quite meet their gaze.

"Wish I'd gotten it off quicker." Remy folds the edge of the wrapper.

"Not your fault." I reach to nudge his shoulder.

He offers a tight smile. "Doesn't mean I haven't been turning it over and over since, trying to figure out what I could have done differently. Maybe stopped it from hitting you in the first place."

"Same," Dejan says quietly.

Cieran doesn't say anything, but he was pulverized on the other side of the field, stabbed and beat half to hell. He's probably got his own memories he's dealing with along with a host of others.

"You both did—have been doing—more than enough. Sorry I checked out."

"You're arrogant and self-centered, can't forgive you." A faint grin tilts Dejan's mouth.

"Never once taken care of us." Remy shakes his head.

"Leaves people hanging out cold every time," Cieran says.

I huff a slight laugh. Somehow the words are more comforting than if they'd actually said what they meant. Dejan's fist against my knee brings the threat of a lump to my throat. He's never this emotive. He really must have been worried, and somehow, even after four years of serving with him, it surprises me.

"Quit acting like I'm about to die," I tell him, a faint smile twitching. A broad one spears his angular face, and in it, I can see the relief plain and clear.

"Who else is going to stop me and Remy from killing each other?"

Remy's deeper laugh joins ours, and it seems like he also relaxes a fraction. Coming from a big family, it's always been like they're the younger brothers, and I'm the older, looking out for them and keeping them in line with a look or joining right in. Though it still doesn't make it any easier to be the one looked after for once.

Maybe I shouldn't always take on the mantle. A soft chuckle draws my attention back to Cieran.

"I used to be a brother," he says. *I get it.* Whatever it was he saw in my face, or slight posture change that maybe the others didn't.

"Still are," I tell him. His eyes are suddenly bright and he swallows hard and breaks off my look.

He's lost family, lost his crew, but that doesn't negate any past relationship. I'm still not entirely sure if he wants the three of us, but he'd be folded into the crew without a second thought if he'd just decide.

But an "O'Donnell," catches his attention and Cox picks his way through the shattered glass. Cieran hesitates only a moment before going to join the other sergeant.

Dejan leans forward and takes another piece of chocolate, and this time I take Remy up on the silent offer. Then it's just the three of us sitting in silence as we wait for the "all clear," and signal to go home.

21

NADIRE

I FIGHT BACK A new rush of tears at the mess around me. For once it's not a mess that'd been brought on by not asking for help. Someone had come to help and this is what'd happened.

Just as fast, I mentally slap myself. About all I could do was wish a sorcerer had chosen a different stomping ground to exact revenge on my brother.

Maya shuffles through some of the destroyed counter and comes up with two cups from the lower shelves that had escaped most of the destruction and undead dust. She fills them with water.

"Here." She presses one into my hands.

"You okay?" I ask. Faint tremors seem to have taken up residence in my hands now that I'm standing still and the threats are gone. She holds up her hand that is similarly afflicted.

"Maybe?" A choppy laugh jolts from both of us before we tap cups together like we're conquering heroes and not just mildly traumatized baristas. "You?" She turns it back to me.

"Feeling one hug away from crying?"

She sets down her cup and goes for it, despite my grumbled protestations. But I return the embrace and I feel steadier when she releases me.

"This is going to be such a mess." I rub my forehead, frowning when my hand comes away smeared in dirt and sweat. Great, I bet I look *real* good right now, too.

"I'll provide moral support when you file all the paperwork?" It comes as a question from Maya, along with raised shoulders and apologetic face.

"Thanks." My own posture breaks.

"This is your shop?" A new voice breaks in, and the unfamiliar woman who came in with Besim's team is there. Her dull copper colored armor matches the slight sheen in the braid coiled around her head. Even though she'd been doing all the fighting and stabbing, she doesn't look much the worse for wear.

"Yeah. Hopefully is going to stay my shop." Another rush of frustrating emotion rushes through me and tries to clog my voice. If I have to pay out of pocket for this stuff, no amount of peppermint mochas is going to recoup that. And goodbye coffee shop.

A wince creases her features, and there's something extra sharp about her cheekbones and the way the light glints off the tinge of copper in her dark eyes that has me betting she's a shifter of some kind. And one of the dangerous ones.

"I only have forty-eight hours' leave time, or I'd be here to help clean up some of the mess I also made."

"You're not part of the Drax Guard?" Maya asks.

The woman laughs, some wild delight there. "No, a different sort of dragon team."

I'm afraid of what *that* means, since dragons haven't been seen in the Americas for a few hundred years.

"But I am heartbonded to Cieran."

I almost clasp my hands together like a little girl. Heartbonds aren't rare, but they're not common either, and knowing someone has one still makes me feel giddy.

"I perhaps invited myself to this fight." Her grin is still in place, and she has no regrets. "I am Athina Spera."

I take the proffered hand and Maya introduces herself next. Athina's attention swings back to me. "Besim's sister?"

I nod. "You know him?"

"My fleet fought with Cieran's team in the Wastelands only weeks ago. That's where we met." She casts a glance over her shoulder to where the sergeant talks to the other officer by the main entry door that's lopsided on its hinges.

"Oh, I don't know if they're *his* team yet..." I stammer.

Athina scowls, eyes narrowing and like Cieran can feel it, he half turns and sends her his own little glare.

"They will be," she says darkly, and Cieran turns again to shoot her the same look.

The other sergeant laughs and points to Athina. "This her?"

"Yes." Cieran sighs and leads him over. "Athina, this is Sergeant Adrien Cox, thorn in my side for the last five years."

Cox chuckles and shakes Athina's hand. "Great to meet you. He's a good one, but if you ever need dirt on him, just let me know."

Cieran rolls his eyes as Athina chuckles. They move off and Athina joins them after a nod to us, and fall to a different conversation. I sit back against the counter, Maya beside me in comfortable silence.

Besim's with his team, and the sight of all three of them sharing the chocolate bar in silence makes me smile. The way he sits is more relaxed, and whatever conversation they'd had earlier has eased something about him. He's closer to the brother I remember before the Wastelands mission.

It seems like two seconds but still an eternity before Cieran announces that we can leave. Maya and I have to go back to the command center to debrief before we can go home.

And when he asks how we want to get there, Maya awkwardly rubs hands against her dusty jeans.

"The last bus that usually takes me home left its stop about two minutes ago, so..."

Cieran immediately looks like it's his fault. "Someone will take you home, put a guard too if you want."

"Won't say no to a ride." Maya smiles and we all start to move.

Dejan hauls Remy up to his feet and the warlock shakes out his hands before moving them in some exact pattern, sending all the shattered glass sweeping together into piles and clearing the way for us to walk out without having to watch our step.

Remy looks one breath away from apologizing again, but I wave him off, thanking him instead for doing a cleaner job than a broom would do.

I find my keys and purse, still safely tucked in the employee area, and when Besim offers to drive, I gladly hand over the keys. Maya claims the backseat, awkwardly sharing at first with Besim's longsword.

He messes with my perfect driver's seat alignment but faithfully promises to put it back. It's nearing eleven o'clock, but feels like it should be the early morning hours at the very least. A few soldiers are still on guard, patrolling the area now roped off with caution tape. As we start to leave, two start putting plastic sheets over the gaping windows.

I refuse to look too close because I might start to cry, and I'd rather save the blubbering mess for when I'm in bed and underneath a pile of blankets.

My first time in the Drax Guard command center turns into a blur. I'd been tired before getting held hostage, and now that adrenaline has officially faded, my body is going into *must sleep immediately* mode. I talk to their CO, an intimidating man who manages to not make me feel like an idiot for letting a terrorist walk into my coffee shop. Twice.

And when we're all done and escorted back to the lobby, Besim reappears. Weapons and armor are gone, but he's still in fatigues and long-sleeved grey shirt. The blood is cleaned from his face, and there's a scab where there had definitely been a clotting wound before.

"Ready to go home?" he asks.

My apartment suddenly seems very quiet and sparse, and he gives an understanding smile when I say, "How about *home*?"

He's going that way anyway, back to his tiny apartment over the garage. And also hopefully a shower because now that he's right next to me...

"Deal with it until we get home. I didn't feel like taking any more time here," he says.

"That I can agree with," I reply, leaning against his arm for a second. I leave his side to hug Maya when her escort appears. Some other guy who looks intimidating enough to be in the Guard, and someone Besim recognizes which reassures me greatly.

"Let me know when you get home," I tell her. "And please don't spend the next days off studying."

She cracks a smile through a yawn. "Tests are next week, so no promises. Let me know when *you* get home and when you'll need help putting stuff back together."

"I'll let you know after I sleep for two days," I say wryly.

She offers a smile again, and turns one to Besim. "Thanks," she tells him.

"Take care," he replies, and I'm too tired to try to tease when it seems like he's watching her leave.

I'm dozing in the passenger seat when he pulls to a stop in front of the house. Lights are still on, and I realize belatedly that it's Friday night and they're still probably watching a movie. We trek up the four broad steps to the dark green front door, flanked on either side by box hedges. He just hands me my keys and pulls out his three keys instead of trying to wade through the mess of my keychain.

I manage an eyeroll which he ignores and pushes open the front door, ushering me first. A breath eases from me once inside the broad foyer, paved in cool tile and built of blocky stone my dad quarried himself.

The stone winds through the house, easing something in all our bones, more so for him, the full-blooded troll, linked fully to earth and stone. It's always made me feel *better* to be in the house, for many reasons, but the city is busy asphalt and concrete and brick, and nothing like the solid steadiness of stone.

"Bes, is that you?" Mom calls and the TV pauses.

"And Nadi," he replies.

Her footsteps brush across the tile that pervades the house, followed by Dad's heavier tread. And when she rounds the corner to the foyer, she comes up short.

"What happened?"

Dad's concern hovering at her side seals it for me, and I burst into tears, hurtling forward into her arms.

"Everything okay?" Taron skids around the corner, Lars a step behind.

"Yeah." Besim's voice rumbles above the sobs shaking through my chest. "Let's go sit down."

It's officially late by the time the story is told, tea and hot chocolate finished, whatever movie they were watching long forgotten, and the fire banked.

Taron and Lars look at Besim with something like awe, and I understand why he doesn't talk about a lot of stuff with us. There's no way to distill all the weapons and fights and magic thrown around in chaos for someone in the comfort of a living room. That's why we only get the fun stories, the buddy moments.

And I'm really glad he has Remy and Dejan, hopefully Cieran too, people who understand it all.

Besim turns in first, saying tired goodnights and leaning over to gently tap his forehead against the top of mine where I'm still sitting next to Mom. I grab his hand and he just nods. He doesn't need me to say thank you again. He'll be there for me whenever I need. I hope I convey something of the same back to him, and the smile that this time reaches up around his eyes tells me he gets it.

Then he's gone through the kitchen and the door leading to the enclosed stairs running between the garage and the house, up to the small apartment he's taken over since joining the military.

Mom and I go upstairs to my old room I used to share with Astrid. Our beds and some old high school décor are still there. Some clothes were purposefully left behind for any impromptu overnight visit, even if we all live in the same city. I pull gym shorts out, though I bum a T-shirt off Taron to sleep in. Mom gets clean sheets out while I duck into the shower and scrub off the dirt and brush my teeth.

One more hug, and the short little blessing they used to pray over all us kids before bed, and then she shuts off the overhead light, leaving the small bedside lamp for me. I crawl into bed, clicking off the light before pulling the blankets over my head and passing out with the next tired blink.

22

Besim

A DULL RUMBLE BREAKS through the depths of sleep. I ignore it, but it comes again, and then escalates to shaking that jolts my eyes open. Taron leans over me and when he sees my eyes open, he steps back.

"What?" I mumble sleepily, ready to pull the weighted blanket back up over my head.

"The guys are here," he says, voice slipping in and out of a deeper tone. I don't remember those days fondly.

"Guys?" I rub grit from my eyes and don't move.

"Your crew, Bes." Taron rolls his eyes.

I blink, lifting my head from the pillow to check the clock on the bedside table. It's just turning nine a.m.

"And the new sergeant guy. I can't remember his name." Taron shrugs.

"Cieran?" I flip my phone over to check, but no messages or missed calls.

He shrugs again. "I guess. Are you getting up or not?"

"They say why they were here?" I start to shove blankets away, a rush of cold breaking through.

"No. Mom's making breakfast."

Okay, nothing urgent then. "Toss me that sweatshirt." I wave across the small room to the narrow window seat where things tend to get left.

As he grabs it, I sit up, discovering a tender shoulder and bruised ribs despite the bit of magic Dejan used last night to kickstart the healing process. My ident tags tap against my bare chest. Taron slowly hands me the sweatshirt, guiltily jerking his attention away from all the scarring visible across my skin.

I pull on the grey sweatshirt, faded letters declaring ARMY across the front, covering all but the scarring on my hand and my neck and face.

"It's okay," I tell him, finally feeling like I mean it.

But he still shuffles sock covered feet, hands stuck in sweatpants pockets. He's lanky and thin for his age, a high school hockey shirt hiding some of it. But like the rest of his brothers before him, he's one of the biggest and bulkiest in his class.

"Are you really doing okay?" he blurts out, red rushing over his cheeks as he manages to make eye contact with me.

Even the fifteen-year-old was seeing it, but he's always been observant and attuned to people. Probably comes with being the youngest of eight kids.

"Yeah, promise."

He tilts his head, not quite believing it. He was around a lot at the hospital, admitting to skipping practice a few times to come sit with me—a sacrifice since he loves sports while still thinking he might have a religious vocation. We talked about a lot in the hospital.

I stand up, rotating my shoulder, neck cracking as I tilt my head to the side.

"Hey." I reach out, snagging an arm around his shoulders. "Promise. Beating up bad guys last night helped a lot actually."

This was the first day in weeks I've woken up feeling…calm.

Taron shakes his head, reluctant smile in place before giving me a one-armed hug. I nudge him away, telling him I'd be down in another minute. I don't bother changing out of the long athletic shorts I slept in or the sweatshirt, just making sure my hair is all sticking in the same direction before making my way down the narrow staircase and into the kitchen.

The tiles are cool, but the heat from the broad fireplace has seeped through the rest of the house, hitting the rune-marked stones through-out the house for extra pockets of warmth as you pass.

Cieran stands in the combined kitchen and dining area, still in a thick jacket, but no hat in sight. He must have sensed my mom hates hats in the house. Dejan sits at the long wooden table, coffee in front of him, thick hair barely tamed. Also, no hat. He learned a long time ago to take it off at entry. Now he doesn't even bother to wear one over. Remy's in the wide kitchen, partially cut off from the dining area by a serving bar, chatting with Mom, and likely trying to coax a new recipe from her.

Attention swings to me as I step in, three sets of eyes scrutinizing, and I shake my head.

"The point was made last night," I say and get varying smiles back. Nothing like driving the point home and making sure I really am okay.

Taron watches from where he's sitting on the back of the couch dividing the dining from one of the living rooms. Until Mom clears her throat and he slides off.

"Cieran." I'm surprised to see him here, especially since Athina's in.

"That's 'Sergeant' to you," he says, but it's mock sternness. I arch an eyebrow and Remy and Dejan's attention swings on him.

"You in?" Dejan asks, barely beating Remy to it.

"Yeah. Told CO last night before I left," Cieran says.

"Good." I nod, and another piece feels like it settles inside.

Mom hands him a coffee mug, and I get one next.

"Where's Athina?" I ask, since he's making no move to leave as fast as he can.

"She's staying on base. I'll go get her in a bit." Making time for me and us first.

"On base?" Dejan's tone is filled with surprise.

Cieran moves awkwardly, staring at his mug for a moment. "Yeah. Got enough to figure out with all this, we didn't want to add in ramped up emotions by staying together."

Mom makes a slight noise of approval, and it gets a faint smile from me. This is probably only the second time she's met him, but now he's announced he's sticking around, she'll be well on her way to adopting him too.

He's not offended, just shoots a wistful look her direction.

"You staying for breakfast, Sergeant?" she asks. "Waffles and bacon."

Her smile falters and I refocus on Cieran, who looks like he's about to get run over.

"I can make something different?" she hastily says, and that breaks him out of it. We're all locked on to him now, but he just shakes his head, clearing his throat in a condemning way.

"No...no, it's just, uh..." He has to take another breath. "My old crew and I would always go get waffles and bacon morning after a mission. No matter what." And it's us three encompassed in the short look he tosses around. "Haven't really been able to eat breakfast since."

Mom moves around the bar and engulfs Cieran in a hug. He holds his coffee mug out to the side to prevent it from spilling all over the both of them, but other than that, not seeming to mind the embrace.

"You don't have to," she says as she steps away, perfectly at ease hugging a near stranger. Guess I get a lot of it from her.

"I think I'd like to," he replies, shoulders finally easing down into something more relaxed. His faint smile appears again, something more genuine that makes the dark circles recede a little more.

Mom pats his shoulder and tells him to go sit down before arguing with Remy long enough for him to convince her to let him make the bacon at least.

Taron joins us at my nod and Cieran starts asking him about hockey. Lars appears, glasses on and hair sticking in all directions. The way his skin alternates between human and stoneskin gives him a ton of cowlicks that have always had him taking the longest in the bathroom.

Dad comes in from whatever he was puttering with outside. Nadi's last down in hoodie and shorts, seeming embarrassed at first to find them all here, but she grabs coffee and takes the seat by me.

"Maya doing okay?" I ask her as she settles in.

"Why are you so concerned about Maya?" She regards me with a teasing look.

I ignore it. "Because she was also held hostage and involved in a fight last night?"

Nadi seems disappointed at the answer. "She let me know she got home last night, and hopefully is still asleep right now. I'll check in a bit and let you know."

But I'm not quite content with that. But *am* content to keep ignoring the *why* for now, instead turning back to the loud breakfast table around me. The crew fits in among my family, another set of brothers who know the more real sides of me than the others do, and won't judge me for them.

They're still checking on me throughout breakfast, small glances my way. I acknowledge every time, wordlessly reassuring I'll be okay, and might be quicker to talk about it if not.

But the slight itching in my skin remains. Once they leave and the house falls back to some quiet, I grab my phone and find the number, pausing for a second before composing a text.

-Hey, this is Besim. Hope it's not weird that I still have your number from you calling the other day. Just wanted to make sure you're doing okay after last night.-

Maya doesn't give me time to overthink any of it, replying immediately.

-Doing okay. Barely slept and am getting a head start on a Starfall: Origins *rewatch instead.-*

-My respect for putting yourself through the end of season one again.-

A laughing face precedes the *-At least I don't have to wait for the next season. Could basically be therapy, right?-*

A smile cracks my face, and I hesitate a moment more, for once feeling unsure about how to proceed.

-Let me know if you need anything.-

-Will do. Thanks for checking in. And for saving our butts last night.-

I don't really have anything else to say other than, *-You're welcome.-* before tossing the phone down. This is the one thing I'm *not* telling the guys about, not even my family, since I'm not quite ready to fend them off if they even get a whiff that I was texting someone other than them.

Maybe I should take some advice from Remy.

A banging on the door announces Taron back. "Street hockey, let's go!"

I shake my head. I might still be sore and exhausted from the last few days, feeling tenuously put together on the inside, but Taron and I can still beat siblings and any neighbor kids at street hockey.

"Okay, give me a second."

Dad meets me in the garage. He's hauled the door up, and stands with hands in jeans pockets as he overlooks the driveway.

"Bes," he says, and I go stand next to him. It takes him a second before he frees a hand and sets it on my shoulder. "I don't say I'm proud of you often enough, do I?"

I half-smile. Dad shows it plenty of other ways, but that's not really it. "You don't have to."

He shakes his head, pulling me into a hug. I lean against him, borrowing some of the steadiness he taught me to wear. And when he gruffly clears his throat, I smile again, not saying anything as he releases me. I tip my head, and he squeezes my shoulder. The wordless affirmation for what I do means more than anything he could have said.

Lars and Taron tumble through the door, feinting around fake punches. A truck pulls up and Enver gets out, striding easily up the drive to join us. My older brother studies me a second, then slaps my shoulder, pulling me in for a quick, rough hug. Mom probably gave him the update on his way over.

I'm more settled, feet steadier against the ground. And as they turn to getting out the gear and dividing up teams, I take a second to call my stoneskin. It rushes over my entire body, anchoring solidly until I release it.

When I look up, Nadi's there. Her smile when she sees the stoneskin holds relief and some understanding. Then she turns away, grabbing a hockey stick. Dad tosses one to me, and we head out.

23

Nadire

Bleak grey light sneaks through the plastic window coverings snapping against their restraints. Clouds moved back in overnight, presenting a gloomy Monday morning for me to finally return to the *Fox and Ground* and survey the damage.

It's somehow better *and* worse than I remembered from Friday. The tarps are the only sound besides my sneakers squeaking against the ground as I set my purse on the counter and move to stand in the center of the café, arms tucked tight across my chest.

Any whole and happy feelings from spending most of the weekend at the house evaporate in the chill. I'm not even sure where to start while waiting for the insurance agent. Finding paperwork? Sweeping up the glass still piled up?

The back door swings open and I whirl to face it, hands clenched like I'm going to fight whoever comes through. It's Maya.

I'd told her I'd be coming by this morning, but that she didn't have to come. Her keys clatter down next to my purse and she slides hands in her jacket pockets.

"Where are we starting?"

I don't answer because there's another sound from the front. Dad carefully opens the door still tenuously hanging on to its hinges. He looks it up and down and then props it open to let some of the light in...as well as all my brothers and Astrid.

A lump pushes up from my chest into my throat and I have to consciously keep my voice even to ask, "What are you all doing here?"

"You think I'd let you hire anyone other than Antilles Construction for this?" Dad sweeps his hand around. "I've got windows in the truck and plenty of hands."

I shake my head and go over to hug him.

"All right." Astrid claps her hands. She's in jeans and boots and has some thick gloves tucked into her work vest pocket. "Where do we start?"

They're all looking at me and Besim has that annoying "see?" expression on his face. I stick my tongue out at him, and start assigning sweeping duty, sorting out broken furniture duty, and turn over the repair work to Dad.

The insurance agent is through next, an older woman with coffee thermos and tablet in hand. She goes around with me, snapping pictures and halting progress at some points for a more thorough inspection. But she's optimistic and by the time she leaves, I already have an email with most of what we talked about and the forms I need to look over and sign.

When I catch Dad alone for a second, he gently cuts off my attempts to ask how much the windows and door and some drywall repair and labor are going to cost.

"Lunch will cover it today."

"Dad." I frown at him.

"Nadi." He gives it right back. "Don't stress about it right now. I want you to be able to get back up and running. Come talk to me after the insurance comes through, and we'll work the family discount."

"*Dad.*" I'm about to cry again, but he hugs me and then nudges me back to work.

"Hey, I need someone tall," Maya calls and pauses, arms still stretched overhead where she's trying to get to a piece of chair lodged on top of the raised wall cabinets. "Which would be literally any one of you guys."

I'm about to head over there but Besim is somehow closer and goes to help. I feel slightly vindicated as they fall to talking easily as he helps her move equipment on the counter for her to wipe and sanitize.

Astrid sidles over to me, broom in hand, and nudges my shoulder. We both exchange a smirk at the sight of Besim and Maya working together. There's a suspicious amount of laughter coming from over there, but maybe we'll pause on the teasing for later since he seems to be more himself.

I grab the industrial sized trashcan Dad and Enver brought, and drag it over to the bigger piles Astrid has created. I glance up as I crouch to hold the dustpan while she sweeps glass into it.

"Um...you can say no if you want." Great start, but Astrid doesn't pause, just waiting for me to get it all out. And I need to. "Taxes are kind of freaking me out, and I could use some help with the bookkeeping and stuff, sometime."

It's the worst way to ask that, but it also came out a little breathless like asking for help is the most nerve-wracking task.

Astrid just smiles and waits for me to dump the dustpan. "I'd love to. Seriously, whenever you want."

I position the dustpan again. "Thanks."

Despite the events that caused them all to be here today, it's still bringing a sense of *whole* I've been missing for a long time. A bit of sunlight breaks through, spearing through the window that Dad and

Enver are placing. Dad's teaching Taron as they go, my youngest brother all focus as they guide it in.

It's missing the café logo, but I can add that back later. Right now, it's one of the most beautiful things I've ever seen.

The End

THE SERIES CONTINUES...

Conduit

WARLOCK SPECIALIST REMY KALAMA will do anything to protect his four-year-old son. And that includes never telling him or anyone else about the fae ex who wrecked his life and violated his sense of self and trust. But secrets never stay hidden, and when his ex, Maeve Ballagh, resurfaces as part of a magic trafficking ring, he and Crew Six are called to bring her in. The kicker? Remy's the bait.

He and his fire magic are ready this time. He just wishes he could trust the crew's new partners.

Half-elf Agent Sara Alder would prefer to stay a data analyst for the Bureau of Magical Affairs, but her boss has other ideas. Her trial run as a field agent shoves her onto the trail of a dangerous fae targeting men with magical abilities. Her job? Solve the mystery and keep Remy's son safe while he and his team take down Ballagh.

When Ballagh gets the drop on the team and vanishes with Sara and the kid, Remy and his team will stop at nothing to get them back. Fae magic is powerful, but he's not alone this time, and it won't take his son.

Acknowledgements

I love this book a lot. And sometimes that surprises me with how much I doubted the entire concept. Write an entire book with alternating sibling POVs in a genre/style that's usually focused on romance?? I don't think I knew how much I needed this book when I started to write it, and edited it over and over. It took talking with a friend who read a draft for me to realize that this one was a "for me" kind of book.

This one is for my family of seven siblings and incredibly supportive parents. We always say that we might not always get along, sometimes get into spirited debates and disagreements, but at the end of the day we still love each other and will go to war for each other. Sometimes sibling relationships can be rocky, and sometimes they're easy. Sometimes they're not talking for months with life and living on opposite sides of the state. And sometimes it's staying up too late camped out in the living room, or perched throughout the kitchen laughing our faces off. Sometimes it's hugs while one cries, sometimes it shadow-boxing and wielding invisible lightsabers in mock battles even though we're all adults now.

And Fates, I wouldn't change it for the world.

So this one is for my siblings, for my parents. For anyone who understands the "who hurt you?" but make it siblings. And for anyone who wanted to see a Catholic character done right.

Special thanks goes to Jenni and Brigitte for beta reading and sending reacts and feedback and always helping me see my books in a little less critical light. For the encouragement and friendship. Thanks to Mollie and Gillian who've been incredible supports and shoulders to lean on, friends to pray and talk and have coffee with.

Thanks to the readers who've supported this series. I hope you're ready for more missions, because the team's just getting started.

And always thanks to the Creator Who's given me this gift and sent the people I needed every step of the way.

More Books by C.M. Banschbach

The Drifter Duology

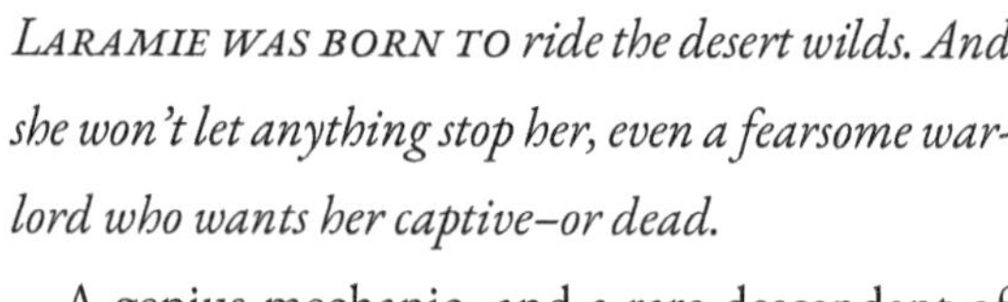

LARAMIE WAS BORN TO ride the desert wilds. And she won't let anything stop her, even a fearsome warlord who wants her captive–or dead.

A genius mechanic–and a rare descendant of the once-magical Itan–Laramie drifts from dusty town to dusty town in search of the family that was taken from her.

But her rambling desert journey becomes a game of survival when Laramie crosses a ruthless warlord's territory. Taken prisoner by one of the warlord's biker gangs, she befriends a quiet, dangerous man named Gered. After surviving hellish circumstances Gered is tired of fighting for a better life.

Laramie will always fight. And she'll stop at nothing to win their freedom.

Enjoy this pulse-pounding motorcycle adventure in a post-apocalyptic western setting with found family and being brave in brutal circumstances. Complete series available!

The Spirits' Valley Duology

A man born for war. A bastard raised in contempt. Only together can they defend their tribe from slaughter.

Fierce-hearted Comran is the chief's son and the favored choice to be the next leader. Then his father chooses Comran's half-brother Etran for the role, straining the loyalties of the tribe and reinforcing the distance between the two men. When Comran is offered the role of battlewolf, he is ready to do his duty—but expects no friendship in return.

Steady Etran has long been shunned as the chief's bastard. Becoming the chief brings even more hostility, so he offers Comran the title of battlewolf to maintain tribal unity. But can he trust this reckless warrior as his general when Comran has never stood by his side?

As tensions mount within the tribe, a traitorous act leads to war. Comran and Etran must overcome their inner demons and fight for their brotherhood before the Greywolves fall to their worst enemies.

Read now!

———

Subscribe to C.M. Banschbach's newsletter for free short stories and book/publishing updates!

About C.M. Banschbach

C.M. Banschbach is a native Texan and would make an excellent hobbit if she wasn't so tall. She's an overall dork, pizza addict, and fangirl. When not writing fantasy stories packed full of adventure and snark, she works as a pediatric Physical Therapist where she happily embraces the fact that she never actually has to grow up.

She writes clean YA/MG fantasy-adventure as Claire M. Banschbach.

Facebook – @cmbanschbach

Instagram – @cmbanschbach

Website (books and merch)– https://clairembanschbach.com/

Newsletter (routine updates and access to exclusive short stories)– https://c-m-banschbach.kit.com/0134a85703